SHAKESPEARE'S HEIR

SHAKESPEARE'S HEIR

Chris Crowcroft

Last Case for Richard Palmer, Investigator

AESOP Modern
Oxford

AESOP Modern
An imprint of AESOP Publications
Martin Noble Editorial / AESOP
28 Abberbury Road, Oxford OX4 4ES, UK
www.aesopbooks.com

First edition published by AESOP Publications
Copyright (c) 2018 Chris Crowcroft

A catalogue record of this book is
available from the British Library.

First edition 2018

ISBN: 978-1-910301-59-3

Printed and bound in Great Britain by
Lightning Source UK Ltd,
Chapter House, Pitfield, Kiln Farm,
Milton Keynes MK11 3LW

*For my sister who taught me
that reading did not have to be out loud*

Note: dates used obey the modern calendar not the old, when the year changed after March 25th.

Chris Crowcroft
chris@crowcroft.co.uk

~ 1 ~

'MY UNCLE TWO NAMES...'

How the letter had reached him by the hand of a servant from the Bell Inn, his old drinking hole over by St Paul's, concerned Richard Palmer less than the bad news it might contain.

How old was his goddaughter now? Richard Palmer counted the years as he pulled on his gentleman-pensioner's gown in time for the obligatory morning service in the Charterhouse Chapel. Sixteen, coming on seventeen, he calculated, of an age to marry. Perhaps that's what the letter was about. But why had her foster-mother Jane Davenant not written it?

His mind went back to a hot day on the banks of a river in Oxford, a serving girl in the water, a suicide prevented followed by the premature birth of the author of the letter in front of him. Miracle, that was the name she had been given because that was what she was and what he had called her after washing her motionless little body in the river, which brought her spluttering into life.

He slipped the letter into his gown for reading during the Chapel service. It was years since he had ceased working at his investigator's trade in the service of Robert Cecil, one-time Chief Minister to the old Queen Elizabeth and her successor James Stuart. No sinecure ever came his way, not then and not since the death of the politician a decade ago. Instead, Palmer had been forced to take charity in the twentieth year of the reign of His

Majesty King James, the First of England. He had never
expected to survive into old age, into his fifties.

Gentlemen-pensioners – or brothers as they were
more commonly called in recollection of this old
Carthusian monastery – were housed and boarded here in
Clerkenwell, Palmer's old patch on the northern side of
the City of London. By a combination of wheedling and
bribery – using the last of the monies deposited with a
goldsmith off Cheapside – Palmer had managed to have
his old bed transported the short distance from his
lodgings on Turnmill Street. It was the last remnant of
the Palmer family wealth gathered over centuries in Kent,
all that was left of a manor house and hundreds of acres
of land accumulated by the scores of Palmers lying at rest
under it.

Now he was reduced to attending a daily service
devoid of the incense which these Palmer ancestors would
have expected under the old faith swept away by Henry
Six Wives and its recurring masses for the dead. These
were gravely forbidden, especially here in Sutton's
Hospital designed as it was to be a model of the new
religion. Curious that it had been owned by a family,
Palmer reflected as the Chapel began to fill, the Howards,
most of whom remained deep-dyed Catholics. From out
of this very place they had served up two sacrificial
victims of their own to political ambition and religious
dispute.

Palmer did not dislike the new liturgy, its Book of
Prayer and its Bible in a language which the congregation
could understand. His father would have been horrified –
the holy old fool, Palmer muttered under his breath, who
had wasted the Palmer patrimony in a last stand for the
old faith against the new. Palmer, the son, had no such

illusions. The State rarely martyred the awkward laity these days, it slowly crushed them with fines and expropriations. So it had dealt with Palmer senior and in consequence with his heir who was now a charity case.

He was heir to nothing other than a bed, Palmer reminded himself as he looked around the gathering in church. It was a weekday, attendance obligatory only for the brethren who huddled together in their black cloaks despite May's promise of better weather outside. God help the world if it was depending on *their* prayers! Palmer had little to do with his fellows, most of whom kept their sad tales to themselves. The loquacious few he avoided.

He slipped the letter out and into his prayerbook in order to read it unobserved.

'My Uncle Two Names, I bear sad news. My foster-parents are dead....'

John and Jane Davenant, Palmer recalled with a sigh, more for Jane, handsome landlady of the Crown Tavern in Oxford than for her laconic husband. Grey eyes and a low voice, excellent thing in woman. So now she was dust as the prayerbook euphemistically put it.

'.... and buried inside two weeks of each other.'

They had taught little Miracle to read and write properly, he could see, or Jane Davenant had more like alongside her own brood. Was it the plague? If it was, it was an unsurprising fact of life. He could count three plagues in his time in London, one of which had nearly carried him off back in the heady days of Gunpowder, Treason and Plot. The Charterhouse Cloister was built around a burial ground for victims of the great plague in their forefathers' time. Taxes, plague and death were the only sure things in life.

The memory of Miracle's mother continued to interrupt his reading, enough to make him want to gaze around the dull, damp-wood-smelling scene dominated, on his left, by the Benefactor's tomb. For all his coalmines, property investments and monies loaned to the great and good Thomas 'Rich' Sutton was dust too, buried over there beneath his monument. He had bought the Charterhouse from the Howards, set up his charitable foundation and promptly died Anno Domini 1611 in his eightieth year, eleven years ago, Palmer counted.

What was her name, Miracle's mother, the girl with the pale red hair, a colour Miracle had inherited – at least she had when he had last seen her in childhood? *Ellen*, that was it. The Davenants had taken her in but she had run off with a strolling player. Bloody actors, Palmer growled to himself, who had once moved in their world whenever they quarrelled, not infrequently with politics.

Ellen had died young, inmate of a bawdy house just round the corner, beaten to death by her pimp, a brutal sort who fancied himself as a playwright; George Wilkins – dead or alive? Rotting in hell in life or in death Palmer hoped who had done his best to send him on that way. Wilkins's writing partner *was* dead, that much Palmer did know. William Shakespeare had died in his bed five or six years ago in his large house in his home town of Stratford-upon-Avon, a King's man and a rich one. Such was the news a man might learn at the Bell Inn, Carter Lane where travellers from Stratford regularly stayed.

Palmer's eyes returned to the letter.

'My foster-brother William is away in the University, the other children will be provided for but there is nothing for me, foster-daughter as I am. I am to go on the parish if I do not marry a certain man I do not want. The gold you sent for me...'

Slim golden angels, Palmer remembered across the years, half-pounds. How he could do with them himself! He had no money these days, not even for visits to the Bell Inn.

'... there is no proof it is mine. There is nobody will care for me. Come for me Uncle, only you can help me now!'

Palmer closed the prayerbook with a sigh. What could he do, how could he help? Obstacle after obstacle presented itself – permission for leave of absence from the Preacher, the priest-in-charge – unlikely. Money for the journey, food and lodging, fourteen shillings at least, twenty to be safe – non-existent. Where could he get it from?

His glance strayed to the Alderman's widow, a daily presence in Chapel. Once he had followed her, paid by her husband as she slept her way round the actors of London. Now she was wrapped up to the gills in black, a middle-aged relict pursing her lips at the sight of anything young and fruity. It would be a pleasure to blackmail *her*, Palmer reckoned.

Who else could he tap? Cecil was dead, his old official too, source of Palmer's Government work, disappeared likely dead. Palmer's one-time employer Sir George Buc, Censor-in-chief had gone mad weeks before in March and wasn't expected to live. As for Henry Lord Southampton, the fair young youth of Shakespeare's sonnet spring thirty years ago, he'd turned Puritan and was acting in political opposition to the King. In any case he had reasons *not* to remember Palmer with gratitude.

How about the actors? Pompous old John Hemmings, he was still around, no longer on the stage, still taking a nice cut from his shareholdings in the outdoor and indoor theatres, the Globe and the Blackfriars. And Shakespeare's first publisher Richard Field, he was doing very well thank you in a new shop and rising high in the Guild which regulated his trade, the Stationers' in Ave Maria Lane.

Emilia Bassano, Mrs Lanier?

Palmer tried to shut her out of his head but she would not be refused. Husband dead, the one whose nose Palmer had squashed in retribution, her son no better than a jobbing musician, she herself, ambitious Emilia last heard of running a school; Emilia a dominie for God's sake who had once commanded the cocks, there was no other way of putting it, of a great officer of state, the poet of the age and a pretty- boy aristo all at the same time!

Palmer was not hopeful. He was in need of a miracle of his own if he was to help his goddaughter.

The interview with the Preacher did not go well.

'You know the terms of your *condition* here,' the priest reminded him.

His tone was as cold as the Chapel in which they were speaking.

A plea that he was being called to act in God's mercy got Palmer no further.

'Her parish priest will see the girl looked after,' was the terse reply he got.

'I ain't goin' on the parish.'

The words of Miracle's unhappy mother Ellen echoed in Palmer's ears across the years. Why would the daughter be any different?

He swore under his breath as he marched away from the Chapel, provoked into a growing sense of revolt. If it meant a leave of absence on his own authority then that was what he would do. The thought encouraged him, a little light rebellion. He hadn't felt so good in months.

But he reckoned it sensible to get the means together first.

'Richard Palmer, alive not dead, by all that's unholy!'

John Hemmings was not happy to see him despite his jovial old mask.

Hemmings was Palmer's second call. In the first it had turned out that the Alderman's wife was nearly as poor as Palmer was and devoted to spending what remained to keeping up appearances. The Alderman had not been as wealthy as he liked to appear, alive or dead.

'He spent his money on informers,' she told him, looking down a long accusing nose at him.

Hemmings was found in Aldermanbury in the heart of the prosperous City of London. Asking around, Palmer was told that he was a widower who liked to be described as 'citizen and grocer'. The fortune he was still making out of the playhouses he didn't like to talk about because of its size, where it came from and the fact that making profit from play was no business for a grown man to the minds of many.

'Why should I?' he said, when Palmer outlined his need for money.

'Because the poor girl is motherless.'

'So are many others. My own children – nine of them, is it? Yes, nine. There were thirteen born, you know – they are motherless.'

'This girl is alone. And her mother died because she left a good situation, one I found for her in Oxford with the Davenants – surely you knew them when you played there?'

Hemmings pooh-poohed the suggestion.

'Barely, the company usually stayed at the King's Head.'

Which was opposite the Davenants' wineshop.

Palmer didn't believe him.

'The girl Ellen was seduced by an actor, one of yours. *He* made it over the street even if you didn't!'

Hemmings had spent most of his life fending off accusations of bad behaviour by actors, too long to be moved by this one. He turned his head away.

Palmer persisted.

'The actor was Ned Shakespeare, your one-time colleague. Brother of the founder of all your fortunes.'

A light flickered in the old actor's eyes, just as quickly extinguishing itself.

'Ned....' he sighed as if that explained it all. 'Not that we don't honour the memory of the great William, of course.'

How, Palmer's eyes appeared to ask?

'Yes, we're working on, thinking of putting together, I mean ... I was just suggesting it to Harry Condell the other day ... a collection of all William's plays. Ben Jonson did it after all and he's still living, the old barrel of lard!'

Lucky to be so, Palmer thought, remembering Jonson's involvement on the fringes of the Gunpowder Plot and his instinct for getting into any trouble going.

'How many plays are there?'

Hemmings waved his hand vaguely at Palmer's question.

'Do you have a publisher?'

Perhaps Palmer could act as a go-between and take a cut from the publisher's fee? He had done as much in his time in the service of the Master of the Revels in his censorship days.

Hemmings headed him off.

'Mr Palmer, we have been dealing with publishers for a generation, we know them all – the good ones, the bad ones, the ones whose word is their bond, the ones who pay what they promise and, above all, the majority who do none of these things. As it happens we have a man in mind....'

Palmer could see he was lying.

'So you won't help me?' he asked.

'She shall be in my prayers,' Hemmings said, giving his solemn stage churchman look.

Richard Field appeared older yet dapper as ever in his shop in Wood Street. His clothes and cut of hair moved with the times, unlike Palmer's.

'That's what you have come to tell me, is it? That the King's Men intend to flog the Shakespeare relics, dead on the stage these last ten years for a profit through the publishing trade?'

Palmer nodded.

'Mr Palmer, I remember our first interview all those years ago, more than twenty, wasn't it? I see you recollect it. I told you then that we did not, nor do we now, touch the works of the stage for all that William was my friend and a fellow citizen of Stratford. A third of our list is works of religion, godly writings. We do publish poetry, thus I published William's first poems in honour of poesy's god....'

... whose apollonian name Palmer doubted Field could call to mind.

Field sucked his teeth audibly.

'... neither you nor I have any appreciation of the stage.'

Field's accusation was true, Palmer admitted to himself.

He had no time for the modern drama which flouted the rules of Aristotle and the masters of ancient classical theatre. As for Field, hadn't he signed a petition against the Blackfriars Theatre when he lived nearby? Despite his 'friend' William being at the heart of the enterprise?

Palmer tried the Ned Shakespeare angle. Field would have none of it.

'If I had to give a shilling for every doxy Ned took his pleasure with, then my wife and stepdaughters would have gone without bread these many years. No, I'm sorry Mr Palmer but I cannot help you.'

So it would have to be Emilia.

Palmer found her closer to than he had expected. Rumour followed by discreet enquiry revealed her whereabouts. She was keeping house for her son the musician a stone's throw away in Clerkenwell, of all the places in the land!

Palmer found the house among the buildings clustered around the parish church of St James, north of the green. Along the street the smell from middens – piles of rotting rubbish and worse – was sweetened by fresh air breezing in from the open country to the north. This hamlet did not feel or look like the City. Why would Emilia, one-time toast of the dark side of the Court, live here?

Palmer kept a careful watch over her comings and goings. How old was Emilia now? Well past fifty, he calculated as he spied on her, dressed like any other London housewife, shopping basket in hand. She had no serving girl with her, a sign of reduced means.

Her hair under her bonnet he saw had turned white. There was no sight of the son, the one she used to claim had been fathered by one of the highest noblemen in the land, her old keeper Hunsdon. That the father was more likely another man, the lowliest of all the candidates – William Shakespeare – was a provenance she would die sooner than admit.

Palmer decided against familiarity.

'Mrs Lanier,' he called out from a safe distance.

She peered myopically in his direction, putting her basket down.

'I thought you were one of the poor brethren walled up in the old monastery!'

Palmer felt discomfited by her jibe. He was used to doing the finding, not being found out.

'Who told you that?'

'Someone who wishes you no good. And your brother's black cloak and hat, they give you away.'

'Who has been talking about me?'

'That would be telling and telling you, from memory, does me no good. Clerkenwell is a small place Richard Palmer, a village.'

Her use of his first name surprised him, surprising him again by pleasing him.

A third surprise was her invitation to enter her house.

He had seen worse. The door led straight into a parlour room equipped with an ancient oak table and a cluster of stools. No master chair indicated no master.

Emilia told him that her school was over and done with as the result of a law case against her landlord full of claims and counterclaims about the state of the building.

'Can you believe my landlord had me detained twice? We could not agree the proper rent.'

Detained? Emilia? Imprisoned, she meant. Nor was she short of other complaints. Her next, she said, would be the recovery of payment for the royal perk her late husband had enjoyed, the old one to do with a tax on the weighing of hay.

'It was assigned to one of my husband's brothers in an underhand way. I was due compensation. I never received it. But I shall.'

Her voice was all triumph-in-waiting.

Was this all that age left us, Palmer wondered, quarrel and dispute? Could this be the beautiful girl courted by him at her keyboard in Kent or the sensation of the half-world close to the Court? What remained of either of them from those Kentish days? She, a put upon disappointed housewife, he a broken-down receiver of charity....

A new arrival interrupted these thoughts.

'I remember you, Mr Palmer, in fact I remember you well.'

The speaker was a man approaching thirty, introduced with pride by his mother as her son Henry, named after the old Lord Hunsdon, cousin, half-brother some said to the old Queen Elizabeth. Palmer took a different line. The man's hair was auburn but thinning, the beard likewise. William Shakespeare's had been the same – another one busy making dust.

'You rescued us on the road to Henley.'

'You helped me repair the carriage wheel,' Palmer recalled and how the boy had reacted, unused to masculine praise never gotten from his stepfather, the one paid to take Emilia and her embarrassing pregnancy off the hands of her elderly keeper. 'What trade are you following?'

Emilia bridled at the word; her son soothed her with a calming gesture of his hand.

'Music *is* a trade. It is one I am proud to follow.'

'Your stepfather did too before he took up soldiering.'

'I owe him nothing other than my name. Music did not cross the threshold, not with him.'

'Your mother played.'

'I owe it more to my uncles, musicians all. The Bassanos and the Laniers have lived in and out of each others' pockets for generations. Sometimes we have sealed the bond with the benefit of clergy, sometimes not.' Lanier smiled. 'My cousin Nicholas Lanier has been my best and kindest master.'

'Nicholas Lanier?'

'He is highly regarded by Prince Charles, our future King,' Emilia quickly explained to Palmer. 'Nicholas also advises His Royal Highness on the painted art.'

'I hope I shall be confirmed a Court musician before very long,' Henry said.

'When a man might have the wherewithal to marry?'

Palmer intended the suggestion gallantly.

'Mother would like grandchildren ... what is your business with us?'

Palmer was reluctant to disclose his need for money in front of the son but he made himself do it and explain why. At the mention of a name, Emilia moved forward on her stool.

'Jane Davenant? Jennett?'

'Do you know her?'

'She consulted Dr Forman, as did I, about ... women's matters,' Emilia said hurriedly to her son before turning back to Palmer. 'She moved away to Oxford with that dull husband of hers.'

Horny old Simon Forman came back to Palmer's mind, he of the stinking breath and an interest in drawing unlikely morals from the plays he liked to attend. Palmer remembered him from the Globe Theatre over the river on Bankside and how he had taken to avoiding him. The Alderman's wife had been one of Forman's clients too – women consulted him about pregnancy or to have their horoscopes cast. Rumour was he liked his payment in kind. Dead too, the old goat, another one making dust.

'We don't have the money you need,' Emilia said. 'But there is someone who might.'

She bent her head towards her son's. Did Palmer hear the word 'Jew'? If he did, it made little sense to him. Jews had been banished for centuries, paying the price, so it was said, for their betrayal of Christ, from generation unto generation – or so the Bible said. Were there really Jews in London?

'Come with me,' Henry Lanier said, 'we have a journey to make.'

It was a long time since Palmer had travelled by boat on the river. Lanier paid the sixpenny fare as they set off together from Blackfriars Stairs on the east side of London Bridge, avoiding the rapids beneath it – they were as likely to tip you into the water as allow you safe passage through. They were bound for Deptford, stopping off point for vessels sailing in and out of London.

The two passengers pulled their cloaks about them to protect themselves from the cold reflecting off the water. The river was busy, at first with smaller boats and then, the further east they were rowed, with larger ones, sails furled, in from every corner of the known world as the colour of the seamen's skins showed and the language shouted in their incomprehensible tongues confirmed.

Lanier had already explained their destination, not one he wanted to be overheard by one of those notoriously chatty watermen who rowed the river boats which were the easiest way to cross London.

'The Bassanos first came from Italy,' Lanier had started by saying, 'from Venice in the time of old King Henry. Some say that earlier they came from Spain.'

It meant little to Palmer. True, Spain had been the evil enemy for most of his own life, the leading Catholic power in Europe determined to invade England in order to extirpate the Protestant heresy – he had fought the Spaniards abroad in his youthful soldiering days. But now that England and Spain were at peace, brokered by King James as his first act in government, Spanish merchants were seen trading in the streets of London. All the same, a powerful cabal in the Court – Lord Southampton among them, one of the trio in the sonnet story which had been Palmer's first case – opposed the long Spanish peace.

'Do you know what the Maranos are?'

Palmer admitted to Lanier that he did not.

'They are Christianised Jews. Faced with expulsion from Spain they converted to Christianity....'

A sensible move, Palmer thought. He himself had switched from the old faith of his father to the new one, the one which was now giving him charity in the Charterhouse.

'... except that some didn't, or only on the face of it. These ones kept their Jewish names privately, made secret wills after the fashion of their Jewish faith.'

The same had happened in England, Palmer knew, in families outwardly conforming to the new faith while practising the old in private. His own father, had he had any sense, could have done the same.

'Are you saying that the Bassanos are secret Jews?'

Emilia a Jewess? Palmer asked himself.

Suddenly it all made sense, this connection with the cursed tribe soaked with the blood of the Christian God pilloried from the pulpit and from the stage so that even an old sceptic like Palmer wondered if there was some truth in the taint.

'I'm saying no such thing. What I am saying is that the Bassano net casts itself wide. They came from Venice, at the crossing of west and east where people blow in and as soon again blow out to all points of the globe. Who knows where they came from or where they will go? Some of our family are talking of going to the New World, to the Americas.'

Henry was conveniently a Lanier, Palmer now understood, French Huguenot in origin so persecuted Protestants, therefore welcome in England. It gave him the safety to say what he did about his Bassano blood. But which was he most, Lanier or Bassano, Christian or Jew?

They found their target in a chandler's shop smelling of rope and grease on the Deptford portside.

Ordinarily Palmer took men as he found them good, bad and indifferent. But what Lanier had told him made him think again. He had run up against and run in black men, mussulmen moors – now *they* were exotic – but this man in the shop in front of him who looked the same as he did, who spoke the same even though Lanier called him 'Zio' – whatever that meant – what was he really? Palmer was wary of this mystery.

One feature of the shop distracted him. In a corner a collection of books appeared out of place, of good quality he judged from their bindings. One might expect books on navigation and travel but the range looked wider when he took a closer look – histories, translations of the classics, even poetry. If Palmer didn't know better he would have taken the man for one who was knowledgeable about books.

'You wish to borrow twenty shillings,' the man said, bringing Palmer's attention back to the matter in hand. 'My charge is a penny ha'penny in the shilling so the total sum to be repaid will be ... twenty-two shillings and sixpence. What is your security? I need to be sure the debt will be met.'

Palmer was at a loss how to answer. Other than the clothes on his back he had few possessions. There was a book of sonnets, Shakespeare's sonnets, worth very little he guessed. The originals in manuscript form which he had claimed back from the printers, mightn't they be worth something? In their time they had generated a publishing fee worth several times what he wanted to borrow today.

'I require something more substantial than poetry,' the man said when Palmer made his offer.

Palmer racked his brain.

'I have only one thing more.'

It was his bed, his ark, the last memento of his family, the best bed in the house, the one reserved for guests when the Palmers had entertained freely in their Kentish manor house.

'With the sheets, pillows and bolsters....'

... the man insisted before he wrote out a contract which he asked Palmer to sign. He counted out the money in bright shilling pieces. Palmer transferred them to a purse which he quickly secreted inside his clothing, a foible ever since he had first come to London more than thirty years ago. He had no faith in belt-dangling purses.

'The debt is due next quarter day, on midsummer day,' the man told him.

Like every other borrower before him, Palmer promised certain repayment.

~ 2 ~

IN ORDER TO SAVE money on the journey to Oxford Palmer faced two choices. The first was to walk. A fitter younger Palmer would have done the distance of fifty miles in two days walking by day and night.

He was neither.

The second was to hire a horse. With an overnight stay the cost might be three shillings in total, two if he travelled without a break.

In either case he must travel alone since time was of the essence. This was not the wisest course what with the risk of ambush on the road from bandits and ruffians.

Palmer looked again at Miracle's letter. It was already ten days since she had sent it on St George's Day, the day they had buried her foster-father a fortnight after his wife. He felt it pulling him towards her. He decided on the hired horse and travelling nonstop. On the back of an old sonnet paper he wrote a letter of excuse to the Preacher announcing a sudden bereavement in his non-existent family.

He was in no mood to study the countryside fresh in its bright May colours as he rode out of London along the Oxford road. The manner of riding soon came back to him even if its effect reminded itself to his rump within the couple of hours it took his horse to walk, trot and canter to Uxbridge.

Ahead of him on the open road he spotted a solitary rider like himself. At first he hung back until he realised that he would be condemned to a slower pace than he needed to make. There was nothing for it, he decided; he would have to take the risk and overtake the man ahead.

As he got closer he saw nothing which aroused his suspicions. The rider was dressed like himself, covered by a large cloak and riding hat. There was no sign of weapons.

Palmer took care not to surprise him by maintaining a steady pace as he came up behind, avoiding the sound of cantering hooves which might create alarm. At a reasonable distance he called out a greeting, one of those sensible precautions of the road. The man turned in his saddle to observe him. Palmer drew up alongside.

'Palmer, it's Richard Palmer, isn't it? Well, well.'

Palmer looked more closely at the other rider.

'And you are?'

'Dr John Hall, physician from Stratford. I never forget a patient.'

Across the years Palmer just about recognised him, the grave awkward young Puritan of thirty now a grave, less awkward, more grizzled man of fifty.

'What brought you to London?' Palmer asked him.

'We have inherited my father's property in Uxbridge.'

The 'we' meant Hall and his wife Susanna, daughter of William Shakespeare. The fear in her face when he was about to take Shakespeare back to London to face the authorities after the rebellion of Lords Essex and

Southampton, Palmer could see it now and how he
hadn't been able to comfort her. Time had healed all; her
father had died in bed, she had married well, the man
alongside him now.

'Mrs Hall is well?'

'She is,' Hall said. 'We have a daughter, Elizabeth.'

'Married?'

Hall laughed, a grating sound.

'She is barely fourteen.'

Girls might marry at twelve, usually the very rich or
the very poor. The reference to youth made Palmer think
of Miracle, two or three years older.

'I must get on,' he told Hall, 'to Oxford.'

'Do you stay there?'

'At the Tavern.'

'Ah yes, the Crown as was. You know the landlord
and landlady have died? Their apprentice is looking after
it, a lad named Hallam.'

Palmer thanked him for the information.

'I attended the deceased,' Hall said. 'He was ill some
months, her passing was more sudden.'

So neither had been helped by the good Doctor?

Palmer was tempted to ask for information about
Miracle but to do so would reveal more than he wanted
to and in any event, was Hall the type to care about a tale
of an orphan foster-child?

'It doesn't sound like the plague,' Palmer suggested
hopefully.

He had an instinct that his own bout with it had
protected him ever since, something he was not going to
discuss with the Doctor. Survivors didn't.

'I do not discuss my patients' illnesses,' Hall said,
'but no, plague it wasn't. It has been in Oxford, it will

come again but presently Oxford is free enough of plague.'

Palmer wanted to discuss it more with Hall, how the disease took hold, why it came and went even, on second thoughts his own immunity from it after it had nearly finished him in Gunpowder year.

Time was against him. He spurred his horse on.

He changed horses in High Wycombe at the cost of a second shilling. Taking nothing to eat he pressed on up onto a long wooded ridge before descending onto Oxford's plains. Afternoon was meeting evening when he rode into the city's centre, at the Cornmarket where the Tavern was to be found.

Palmer found no warning plague circle painted on the tavern doors which were open for business in the usual way. His intention was to stay if invited but old habits made him check it out first.

Inside a young man was acting the part of the landlord, the apprentice Palmer presumed.

'I am looking for Miss Miracle,' he said. 'I am her godfather, Richard Palmer.'

'She's not here.'

Palmer said nothing to this truculent reply. He kept up a steady gaze.

The young man gave in.

'She's been taken in by the parish. She's in the care of the priest.'

Palmer's eyes narrowed.

'And where would that be?'

'St. Martin's, on Carfax.'

'I knew Mrs Davenant. She would never have wanted Miracle to go on the parish.'

'There was no choice, she wasn't in the will. If she had been....'

'She would have made a good marriage prospect, yes? Educated, a dowry from her godfather....'

'What dowry?'

Suspicion and cupidity mixed in the apprentice's eyes.

'... anyway I am promised to Jane Davenant, the third daughter.'

It was the way it usually went, Palmer understood, the apprentice marrying the widow or the daughter in order to keep it all in the family and the business a going concern.

'Tell me,' Palmer asked as confidentially as he could, 'what will the priest do with her?'

The youth looked sly.

'Best ask the Curate that.'

Palmer lost no time in tracking the Curate down. He entered St Martin's Church through a handsome and, to his eye, ancient square tower. Inside he quickly recognised from a plethora of pompous monuments that it was the church of the city fathers, the burial place of Oxford's mayors including, most recently, the laconic John Davenant and his warmer wife. He realised he had been here before when he walked past an old baptismal font where Miracle had lustily protested against her entry into the Christian faith.

The Curate's handshake was clammy, his manner unctuous, his age not young not yet old. Palmer got straight to the point, introducing himself and what he was. He asked to see Miracle.

The Curate appeared to want to be helpful.

'I believe she has gone to the market. Tell me again, who is it I shall tell her wishes to see her?'

Palmer repeated his name very slowly.

'I am sure she will want to see you, only ... that is what I think. Young people, they have minds of their own, don't you find, Mr, er....'

'Palmer, as I said. Tell me, what is Miracle's position here? You tell me she has gone to the market. Has she a place in the priest's household here?'

'A place in the household? I cannot answer that, I am not the Rector. But yes, she is staying here while it is decided what can be done for her.'

Palmer knew what that meant, finding her work as a serving girl or, worse case, consignment by the Overseer to a poor house and rough menial work. He shuddered at the thought. But what more could he offer her? His few shillings would not improve her chances or pay a lawyer to secure guardianship for him to take her away, and to what? A strolling player had taken her mother away to London where her life had turned out nasty and short and all under his eye too. Who was to say that something found for her in Oxford wouldn't be better, far better all round?

'I am surprised she is out of the Davenant family.'

The priest hesitated before answering Palmer's accusation.

'It wasn't Mrs Davenant's doing, she was very fond of the girl.'

'And Mr Davenant? I did not find him unkind to her.'

'Ah, but Mr, er ... Palmer, families are queer things. Mr Davenant had a care for his sons especially the second, William. He and Miracle are of an age, an impressionable age....'

'You mean....'

'I mean ... William is at the University in Lincoln College. His father dearly wished him apprenticed to some London merchant. It is said he inherits one hundred and fifty pounds in the will if he complies....'

The look of envy in the Curate's eye betrayed just how much money that was, ten years' worth of his stipend, maybe more.

'... and the girls inherit two hundred pounds each. It will be a handsome sum for young Miss Jane to set up home with the apprentice.'

But would she want Miss Miracle in their home? The priest's chuckle suggested not.

His sums put Palmer's few gold angels in a cold light. All the same he brought them up, describing them as a christening present.

The priest looked interested.

'Is there any evidence of it?'

'My word as a gentleman,' Palmer shot back. 'I was at the time in the employment of Lord Salisbury, the Chief Minister. I could make a legal statement, an affidavit to that effect.'

'Strange, there was nothing about it in the will. Usually, known debts owed are provided for.'

'Perhaps Mr Davenant did not know about it. I gave the money to his wife.'

The Curate raised a suggestive eyebrow.

'Please pass the message to Miracle that I have come,' Palmer said. 'I will call again in the morning.'

He intended no such thing. Instead, Palmer found his way to the marketplace.

It was almost deserted in the early evening. Here and there stallholders were packing away unsold goods. A handful of housewives stood gossiping.

Palmer went over to a butcher's stall with little left to sell and what there was, unlikely to be fresh after a day in the open air.

'I'm looking for a young woman....'

'Be'ant we all,' the butcher replied in his rolling country accent.

'About sixteen, red-haired I should guess, used to live in the Tavern, name of....'

'Miracle?' the butcher said. 'She was here. Look ... over there,' he said, pointing to a water trough where a figure was sitting, her back to the marketplace.

Palmer approached from a wide angle so that he could catch a better sight of her first. She was playing disconsolately with a dwindling bunch of daisies as if she couldn't be bothered to make a chain out of them. She was the image her mother, Palmer saw, the same slight figure, same pale red hair.

He wanted to let her get a good sight of him before he reached her. He was feeling oddly shy, unsure what he should say. He had little or no experience of young people, girls especially except, in the grimmest of circumstances, arrest and distraint.

She looked up and saw him. Embarrassed she hid the wilting flowers behind her back.

He walked closer.

'Are you...?'

'Yes,' he said. 'Uncle Two Names, but I prefer Richard.'

Miracle burst into tears, enough for the few remaining bystanders in the marketplace to look round.

'I knew ... you would ... come,' she sobbed.

He liked her voice which was not her mother Ellen's, despite the Oxfordshire lilt. It was low and well pronounced like Jane Davenant's. He sat down beside her, both their backs to the onlookers.

'I've been to the church, met the Curate....'

He noticed her shudder.

'I see. Is he the man you mentioned in your letter?'

She nodded her head. Few things disgusted Richard Palmer but this did. Such a man should be looking for a pious wife, a widow perhaps who might bring him her portion. If he was looking at a penniless girl it could only mean one thing and it wasn't Christian charity.

'Are you living with him?'

Miracle shook her head.

'My place is in the Rector's kitchen until it's decided what's to be done with me. Everyone is telling me that the

Curate is a better man than I should rightly expect, that I should be grateful.'

It would be the easy way out Palmer agreed but only to himself.

'No, you're not for him,' he heard himself say.

'It's William I love!'

Palmer took a good guess at who this William was. It was likely the Davenants' second son, the child Jane Davenant had been carrying when Palmer brought Miracle and her mother in from their river rescue.

Miracle poured out his virtues – his looks, his character, even the quality of his dress as a student at the University. As for his ambitions....

'He says it's London and the Court for him, he's no mind to be a merchant such as his father wanted. As for me I should be happy if he was in the meanest place in the world so long as we are together. We're not flesh and blood,' she fired out dramatically, 'he's not my real brother!'

Palmer stood up. Miracle raised herself up beside him, her hand on his forearm. He let her keep it there, it afforded him comfort as well as her.

'I shall have to meet this William,' he told her firmly.

He arranged to meet her in the marketplace tomorrow with William if it could be arranged. Satisfied that she was in no risk for the time being, he left her in order to find himself cheap lodgings with decent beer.

Time to drink and think.

Two tankards of beer in a lowslung alehouse took his thinking no further forward. What in God's name was he to do about Miracle?

Slowly a plan formed. The least he owed her was to put a stop to the Curate's designs on her – if he couldn't do that he wasn't Richard Palmer. As for the golden angels, it would make a difference if he could get hold of them on the grounds that they had been held in trust for his goddaughter. He might try to shame the will's executors – there was usually a lawyer involved and they hated threat of scandal.

But in the end, the wider question remained, where did her future lay? Was there nobody who might take an interest in her, pretty, experienced in the tavern trade, well-spoken and better-lettered than most? He shivered as he thought of her mother Ellen and her dreadful end. Other than her education, the same could have been said about her.

As for this William Davenant, Palmer did not see him as the answer. Her hopes of him would do neither of them any good.

~ 3 ~

HE DID NOT SLEEP well among his snoring, farting fellow guests in the common chamber with its shared lice-ridden beds. He missed his old bed at home so he was happy to be up at dawn, scratching and patrolling the city. He took the chance to visit the inn where Ellen had been knocked up all those years ago by her employer, Miracle's father in case he could dun some more money out of him. Long gone, long dead he discovered, another one reduced to dust.

When he arrived at the Tavern he was surprised to see Dr John Hall at breakfast.

'I had expected to find you here last night,' the Doctor remarked.

'And yet you came here all the same?'

Both men laughed, rare sights.

Other than this they had little to say to each other.

Palmer wished Hall a pleasant day's ride home to Stratford and got up to leave.

The moody apprentice landlord was watching him from beside the bar.

Palmer went up to him.

'Thank you for telling me about the Curate.'

Hallam looked surprised then smirked.

'I shall put a stop to it,' Palmer told him. 'I should also like to speak to Miss Davenant, Miss Jane, your betrothed as I believe you told me....'

'Why would she want to talk to you?'

'I knew her mother, she carries her name, I wish to give her my condolences. There's no *harm* in that, is there?'

Palmer loaded a hint of threat into his tone.

Hallam eyed him suspiciously.

'I suppose not,' he grumbled.

The Curate appeared to know something was in store for him. In Palmer's experience types like this usually turned nasty or scuttled away out of sight.

'I hear you have been speaking to Miracle,' the Curate said.

Miracle had been telling him, Palmer guessed, what her important godfather thought.

'I stand quasi in loco parentis,' Palmer started to say as pompously as he could just to put the Curate on the defensive. 'As such, I see no advantage to my charge in marrying a poor priest without prospects, prospects which might otherwise have overcome her lack of feeling for such a man in a parent's eyes.'

He did not have this status in law, both men knew it. It didn't stop him.

'Should my view be challenged I should be happy to make my case before the magistrates of the town. False imprisonment would be my grounds, a writ of habeas corpus the redress I would seek....'

It was bluff, pure bluff learned from half-digested lessons at the feet of the mighty lawyer Lambarde half a lifetime ago; another one turning to dust.

'... and I will lay this case against the Rector in the first instance since he has taken charge of her.'

The Curate blanched.

'Then you would be happy to see Miracle in the poor house?' he argued back.

'No, I would seek legal guardianship of her, custody at the least pending the decision, to be arranged with respectable friends.'

'That might take years. It might need to be heard in London.'

'... where I live, where I am known as a former servant of the Chief Minister. It will be you against me, I the guardian, you men of the cloth seeking *concupiscence* with this poor young orphan. Have you got the time, the money, the friends? Above all,' Palmer said, lowering his voice and leaning in, 'can you *wait* so long?'

Both men knew what he meant. The Curate swallowed hard.

'Oh for God's sake! I will speak to the Rector.'

Palmer decided to follow his instinct which was to find young William Davenant before he disappeared with Miracle and turned up like Romeo and Juliet before a meddling priest. There will be no potions administered here, Palmer firmly promised himself.

Careful observation of the lodge at Lincoln College, buried among its bigger brethren and a silver groat to the porter on duty gained him the identification of his target. He had only to wait until the boy – and he was a boy –

came out into the street. A boy should be no match for a man.

Palmer accosted him. The lad was handsome in a healthy, youthful way.

'I am Miracle's godfather,' Palmer said.

The claim seemed to create some recognition from the young man.

'... we must speak. Are there private gardens where we might go?'

William Davenant led him back into the College until they found the necessary seclusion.

The boy had a charming smile and used it.

'Miracle told me you had arrived! Great news!'

'I'll come to the point,' Palmer said, cutting him off. 'What are your feelings for Miracle? I'm not speaking as the godfather, think of this as ... man to man.'

Conflicting emotions vied for control of the boy's face.

'She means ... so much to me.'

So, not everything?

'We were babes in arms, twins almost....'

Good, good, Palmer thought, sibling affection but no more.

'Like ... Plato's two halves of the whole, or is that Socrates? She is my other half.'

Not so good.

'Who would not love her?'

Palmer began to fear sheafs of private sonnets already piling up hidden in a college room in praise of 'wondrous Miracle'. He must go on the attack.

'Do you fall in love easily? You're at the age when young men do, there's no shame in it.'

The young man's physical recoil was so graceful it could have been stage-acted. But he gave no answer.

'Have there been other women, are there others?'

Again no answer.

'What are your ambitions, Master William?'

The question unleashed an outpouring, about a life of books and plays, London and the Court – he might start as a page in some noble household ... was he at sixteen too old?

'My cousin Robert, on my mother's side, is the Court perfumer....'

'A servant, William and servants peddle goods and services not influence.'

Not exactly true but the boy was unlikely to know better.

'What about the players, Mr Palmer, the King's Men, we knew them well – I met Mr Hemmings when I was fourteen or so.'

So old Hemmings had been lying about barely knowing the Davenants.

'And what did he say? Come and see us if you're ever in London?'

'Exactly, yes he did,' the boy answered eagerly.

'That's what they always say. There's a young William Davenant in every town they visit, each one with the same dreams.'

The boy appeared crestfallen.

Palmer spoke more gently.

'And where does marriage with Miracle fit into all of this?'

Davenant drew up short at the m-word.

Palmer pressed his argument home.

'You can have her as your sister, William and achieve all these things. But as your love it must mean your wife because – and this is not the godfather talking – it's what she herself will want; think of her mother who didn't and look what happened to her. I saw her mother's end, William, a sad, vicious end.'

And he had, Ellen bleeding to death on the floor of his chamber after a beating by an unspeakable man.

'I cannot lose Miracle.'

Davenant's words were obstinate.

'Can you keep her? There's nothing in the will for her or so I hear.'

'Yes I know,' the boy admitted, as if he had been counting on it.

'Is there an executor?'

'No,' the boy said, 'no there isn't.'

'Then you heirs will have to prove the will.'

'I see. My father – you knew him, I understand – he wanted me to get myself apprenticed to a respectable London merchant; it's there in black on white in the will....'

He pulled a face to indicate what he thought of his father's dying wish.

'... and I'm welcome in the Tavern, for my meals and such but if I and my friends take wine we've to pay for it! Oh he was such a tavern-keeper! I do wonder if he was my father at all.'

'You think somebody else was?'

William's look was coy. Could he, should he tell, it said?

'My parents *loved* the actors, we entertained them in the Tavern whenever they visited Oxford. One, William Shakespeare, yes, *the* Shakespeare, he treated me and my brothers as if we were his godchildren. He stayed as our guest. He showered us with kisses. People say that we, Master Shakespeare and I....'

Palmer struck the boy, a slap around the face.

Davenant fell back, shocked, nursing his cheek reddened by the blow.

'If you were a man not a wretched boy,' Palmer shouted, 'that would have been my fist. Think what you like of yourself or men like this Shakespeare but as for your mother, don't you *ever* bring her reputation down into the dirt!'

The boy continued rubbing his cheek.

'But Mr Palmer, I was only seeking to elevate it.'

Palmer regretted his action. He paced the town centre several times in self-reproach.

It was unlike him to suffer from moral outrage. His own view of life was not so dissimilar to the boy's. Why had he done it? Because Jane Davenant was one of the few people he had ever respected? Did that mean she must be pure? Why? What if she had needed relief from a humourless husband for whom their Tavern and this city were the world?

For Jane read Miracle, he understood in the light of what had happened to Ellen. Doing what you wanted had its costs. What would happen next when he was confronted by the young couple together?

Youth never shaped itself to see sense.

He made his way back to the Tavern in search of Jane Davenant, the daughter.

In one sense, his task was made easy, she was the sister serving in the Tavern today. In another it wasn't because she was busy. Finally she found time to pull up a stool and talk to him.

She was like and unlike her mother.

Physically she was a smaller version with the same grey eyes but her voice was high and tending towards petulance. The second youngest girl, had she been spoiled, neglected, both? He was tempted to think that anyone who would settle for the scowling apprentice Thomas Hallam was no better than she should be; but then hadn't her mother settled for dour John Davenant? Even if John had, according to his wife liked the plays in their London days, especially those by William Shakespeare?

'I suppose we shouldn't complain. It's a good business we have here.'

'Do you think you will take it on?'

'It's what Father wanted,' Jane said without thought. 'My Thomas, he can play the man's part like Father and I shall be like Mother.'

'And there's no room for Miracle?'

Jane pouted.

'She's not our sister, you know, she's not blood. It's not as if Father saw a place for her here in his will and his will was, what's the word?'

'Explicit. Did you not get on?'

'It's not that. I can't say we've ever had an angry word – might have thought it, never said it ... it's just, she was always Mother's little pet.'

'I should think the circumstances of her coming here had a lot to do with that.'

'I was a little girl when that happened, four years old, five maybe....'

Mother's pet herself Palmer wouldn't wonder, her nose put out of joint by the angelic little newcomer.

'Mother said she was, what was it? Our special care sent by God. What will happen to her now? I hear as how you've saved her from the clutches of the Curate! He's asked for me and my sister Alice more than once. But I have my Thomas.'

'So you know Miracle's story....'

'So what if I do? I remember her mother too, Ellen wasn't she? No better n' she should be, Father used to say, ran off with an actor, brother of a friend of Mother and Father. Oh, the angry voices we heard, Mother and Mr Shakespeare, Mr William that is, the friend, not Ned, not him as took Ellen away. It was years before we saw him again, Mr William that is. I hear she ended badly that Ellen. Did she?'

Palmer nodded sombrely at the memory. Ellen was far too present in his mind these last few days, bleeding to death on the floor of his Clerkenwell chamber.

'I expect Mr Shakespeare soon regained favour when he did come back.'

'Oh yes, all the boys liked him and to be fair, he was kind with us girls too. When he came back from London on his way home there was always something for us, for all of us.'

'Was your brother William his favourite?'

Jane gave him an old-fashioned look.

'He's not been givin' you that story of his, you know, about Mother and Mr William? He has, I can tell he has! Oh he's a proper little romancer that brother o' mine. It'll get him into trouble one o' these fine days.'

It already had Palmer reflected but he wasn't going to tell the young woman in front of him in case it caused a closing of family ranks.

'Miracle's story,' Palmer repeated. 'Did your mother ever tell you about the pieces of gold?'

Jane slapped her knees as she laughed.

'Did she ever! Our little angel Miracle given these angels by her godfa ... say Mr Palmer, that wasn't you, was it?'

Palmer wrenched a smile out of himself.

'I suppose your father looked after them.'

'Oh no-o-o! Mother put them with her treasures.'

'Her treasures?'

'Yes, in her trinket casket. She had a few pieces of jewellery and what she used to joke was her runnin' away money. Mind, she only told us that when we was older and could fend for ourselves.'

'This trinket case ... I suppose it went down in the inventory after your mother's death?'

'Oh no-o-o! Well, Father was sinkin' fast too so all that was left for later. In any event we were told that what was hers was his according to the Law....'

Palmer didn't like to ask the question. He didn't have to.

'... the trinket case is with me, I rescued it and put it by. I've been meanin' to look in it, only....'

'It would have distressed you.'

'Oh no-o-o! It's locked, see and I can't find the key.'

Nothing surprised Palmer about human nature including how easy it was to persuade Jane to bring him the casket so that he could open it. Since they couldn't do it on the premises Palmer suggested neutral ground. St Martin's Church seemed as good a place as any, one where a good young woman might safely go without compromising her reputation.

Jane's eyes widened as Palmer took his knife from his boot and fiddled the simple lock open.

'You've done this before!' she giggled.

There were in a secluded place in the nave, out of sight behind a pillar.

'This is just like a play Mother and Father took me to.'

Not another one, Palmer sighed to himself. What was it with plays and women?

He opened the box. Caskets like these Palmer too often found to be melancholy troves having emptied several in his time, dispossessing some poor wretch of a last few belongings under the sanction of the Law. He ignored a little wad of letters on the top in case Mr John Davenant had been a clumsy poet in his wooing or someone else had since. Beneath them, to one side he spotted a mingled pile of uncostly jewels – the odd ring, a couple of coloured gems, a necklace of seashells speckled with pearls warped and fallen away from a broken string. To the right of the divider was a little cache of coins, silver mainly with the odd soft shining of gold. There were no angels.

Palmer's eye fell on a tiny leather pouch. He took it out and opened its strings. He passed the casket over to Jane to examine ignoring her little squeaks of pleasure as she riffled through the box item by trivial item. He opened the purse. There they nestled, tin-thin pieces of golden treasure, enough to give any ordinary girl half a start in life.

A tiny scrap of paper caught his attention. He pulled it out and opened it up.

'Miracle's Bounty,' it read.

He felt a tug at his arm.

'How much do you think these things in the casket are worth, Mr Palmer?'

'Have you counted the money?'

'Yes, there's five marks and more.'

'The jewels will be worth double that,' Palmer lied as he took the casket from her and closed the lid.

Jane was biting her lip. Palmer knew what it meant – do I have to tell my sisters?

'What would be *equitable*,' Palmer started to say, knowing that the word would impress her and give her excuse for what would be anything but legal, 'is that you keep the money – say you didn't find any – and share the jewels among your sisters.'

'What, as keepsakes like?'

'As keepsakes.'

'And ... the gold in the leather purse?'

She was a sharp one and no mistake. Palmer showed her the scrap of paper with Miracle's name.

'How much was it?'

'You know how much.'

'That's handy money, Mr Palmer, ten shillings apiece, half a pound.'

Palmer took her by the hand.

'Here's the deal,' he said. 'You take what I suggest, I keep the angels for Miracle as was intended.'

'But Mr Palmer....'

'I haven't finished yet. I take Miracle away with me, out of the parish, out of your life....'

... and away from the eyes and any wandering hands of the apprentice Hallam, Jane's betrothed.

Jane thought about it.

'It would be better, for my brother William of course.'

'Of course.'

A good day's work, Palmer reckoned as he watched Jane skip happily out of the church.

He had reckoned without the Curate.

'Moneylending in the Temple, Mr Palmer or did I see *stealing*?'

Palmer stood up, an old truculence asserting itself inside him.

'Think what you like, priest but be careful what you say in case you have to justify it in court!'

'Court is more likely where you'll find yourself. What was it I heard? Take Miracle out of the parish? That would be in breach of the legal responsibilities of the Overseer of the Poor. Who will be charged with false imprisonment now? Or should I call it by its commoner term – kidnapping?'

Palmer thought quickly. The Curate had only heard the end of the conversation was his reasonable guess. He put his arm around the Curate's shoulder as he walked them both towards the door.

'It's a moot point, priest. She's in the Rector's care you say so a decision hasn't yet been made? And if a decision hasn't yet been made it means she has not yet been entrusted to the care of the Overseer so his responsibilities cannot have been breached. As to the legal standing of your, I mean the *Rector's* present care of Miracle, the legal position is not very clear is it?'

'What *are* you suggesting?'

'Nothing, only that the Rector might be considered to be in an awkward position the longer his *temporary* care for Miracle goes on. You do see the dilemma, don't you?'

The Curate shook Palmer's arm from his shoulder.

'You haven't heard the last of this!'

Oh yes, I have, Palmer reckoned to himself.

~ 4 ~

I T WAS MIRACLE who brought William Davenant to
Palmer rather than the other way round, on her half
day off. Boy eyed man warily after his bruising
experience on their first encounter.

Palmer walked them for half an hour eastwards to the
spot he had in mind, a bank by the river.

'This was where you were born, Miracle,' Palmer
told her, 'where, in a manner of speaking I baptised you
here in this river.'

And then he told them an edited version of the day's
events. In one sense, it was as if time stood still – nothing
had changed. In another, the intensity of the memory, the
hard heat of the day all those years ago made what he saw
around him appear pallid and indifferent, the same place
but not the same, its divinity removed.

Miracle was clinging to his arm. The boy was
unusually silent.

'There! What do you think of that, Will?' Miracle
asked him.

'Marvellous, wonderful in the telling....'

Palmer caught the classical allusion.

'... what a great scene it inspires, in poetry, in
drama....'

'What? My poor mother giving birth and me all pink
and ... naked?' she whispered modestly.

'Sit down.'

They obeyed Palmer's order, side by side.

'Here's the position,' he started to tell them. 'In front of me, a pretty boy and pretty girl who have barely seen their sixteenth birthdays....'

'I shall be seventeen in three months,' Miracle protested.

'And I six months after,' William said.

Palmer was not to be dissuaded.

'*She* has nowhere to go unless it be the poor house. *He* is a college boy who has yet to take his degree.'

'I shall have one hundred and fifty pounds under my father's will, enough to marry and set up home! Let my brothers be the clergyman, lawyer and whatever, I shall go to Court....'

'... except you are not yet of age. Your father was not so ill that he did not place controls on your access to the money.'

'He allows me forty pounds immediately.'

'*If*, as I've heard, you agree to find an apprenticeship with a London merchant. The money's to pay your master's premium.'

'I shall *never* do that. I am not cut out for trade!'

'So, Master Davenant, in college you must remain.'

The boy half rose to his feet. Palmer pushed him back down.

'What about me?' Miracle asked, faith shining in her eyes that her godfather was about to make all well like in the plays.

Palmer turned his face fully towards her.

'I, Miracle, am what's called a gentleman- pensioner. That means I have a place but little or no money.'

'No money,' she echoed.

'Except for several gold angels.'

He pulled out the little leather purse and showed them the coins. Miracle's eyes shone then faded as she realised how short a time they would last if she was to marry a penniless student.

'Mr Palmer, perhaps I speak with the inexperience of youth,' William said, successfully getting to his feet this time, 'but as I see it, I love Miracle and Miracle I believe loves me.'

'I do, I do,' she murmured to herself.

'You imply that we have nothing besides our love. Well, I dispute that. Miracle has her freedom – those angels buy her that as evidence at least that she has no need to go on the parish. I am the second son of a father lately deceased whose will shows him to have been a wealthy man. One hundred and fifty pounds is marked against my name and it shouldn't be beyond my wit to get it somehow and....'

Words failed him.

Palmer walked to the river's edge. He knelt down stiffly and scooped up a double-palmful of the cold water before splashing it onto his face to cool himself down. He returned to the young couple.

'Here's what we do. William, you stay in college – no buts, you have your father's will to prove as well as finding ways of extracting from it the money you've been boasting about. Miracle, you'll come with me to London.'

'But London, that's a world away!' the boy protested.

'A day's ride for a fit young man. I will find you respectable lodgings, Miracle and if we can, a situation....'

'She's not to be a serving maid. No wife-to-be of mine....'

'... a situation consistent with your upbringing, Miracle. If you, young Will resolve your father's will, take your degree and settle on some profitable course of action in life – which I will be the judge of – then you can start to talk of living happily ever after.'

Behind his back Palmer's fingers were crossed.

Palmer and his goddaughter left Oxford in the early hours of the next morning.

'It's best this way,' Palmer had told her.

He knew that none of the Davenants would follow her nor did the Overseer of the Poor have any authority to. It was down to the Rector and whether he thought she had been abducted. The Curate might encourage him. More likely he would breathe a sigh of relief that Palmer was out of his life and, if he was wise, that Miracle was beyond his temptation.

Palmer picked a sturdy horse from the hiring stable, one capable of carrying two if need be as well as the girl's modest packet of clothes. He counted fifteen shillings left in his purse besides the gold angels. A second relay horse and overnight food and accommodation for two would still leave him ten shillings to the good when they arrived in London, and the gold angels untouched.

Once again he trusted to luck on the open road.

Luck held. Ten miles out they were slowly overtaken by a party, a carter with a group which chose to travel with him for mutual protection. The carter looked an honest man, Palmer judged.

Palmer shook his hand, slipping him a concealed shilling. The man saluted him.

Emilia Lanier was shaken from her half-sleep in front of an empty hearth in the late hours of the evening. Inching open the window shutter she saw two figures standing outside. One she recognised as Richard Palmer. His having a young girl alongside him did not bode well to her mind.

'But why not?'

Palmer argued hard.

Emilia was out of the room having been sent by Emilia to find what food she could in the back-kitchen.

'Because.'

For a second time Palmer showed her the golden angel he was offering in return for lodging for the girl. It was a tempting sum.

'Firstly, I don't have the room.'

'But you admitted that your boy is frequently away following his work. Wouldn't you value the company and the help? You keep no servant.'

'That he is frequently away doesn't mean that he doesn't come home. And it's not seemly.'

Seemly? From Emilia? Palmer laughed out loud.

'Your Henry and Miracle, under the same roof? Plenty of serving girls live under such circumstances.'

'She wouldn't be a serving girl would she? She'd be, I don't know, a guest....'

'A *paying* guest.'

'Then what happens? I know what you're up to Richard Palmer, you think I'll get fond of the girl and then where would we all be?'

'I need time to find her a situation – an apprenticeship where she could live in.'

'And what would you know about such things ... oh, and don't go thinking that I'll help you!'

They were interrupted by Miracle bringing in a wooden platter of bread and cheese.

'I have brought enough for the three of us. Is that all right, Mrs Lanier?'

She was a good girl, Palmer knew and saw that Emilia saw it too.

'Curse you Richard Palmer,' Emilia mouthed silently towards him.

'The agreement over Miracle does not extend to you,' Emilia said later as Palmer pulled his brother's cloak about him ready to go out into the night.

'... you will have no special place here. And it depends on what my son says, which will be decided using his head and not any other part of him, I'll make sure of that.'

'I should think so too. She's a good girl and I'm her respectable godfather!'

'Where will you go now?' Emilia asked him.

Palmer laughed.

'To face the wrath of God's representative on earth.'

Palmer might have risked telling the Preacher the truth had he not wanted to cover his tracks from the authorities in Oxford.

'A long-lost foster-brother,' the Preacher said, pursing his lips, 'went to sea, came back and conveniently died?'

'In Kent,' Palmer added.

'And what evidence is there of this?'

'My word as a gentleman.'

'I see. And the name of the church where he lies buried?'

Palmer gave him one.

'And the priest, his name was?'

Palmer gave him that too, one which was correct except it was forty years out of date.

'I could send to this priest, to the church, have the parish register read to confirm what you say.'

Palmer gave the priest an offended look.

'... and I reserve the right to do so.'

Palmer was relieved. He had won his point.

'Hold hard Mr Palmer! The message you left me, I found there was a sonnet on the reverse. There is no place for sonnetolatry,' – the priest smiled at his own witticism – 'among the gentlemen-pensioners of this noble institution.'

Palmer should have left it there but he could not resist an argument.

'The Dean of St Paul's Cathedral, our mother church....'

'Our revered Dr Donne?'

'John Donne was a mighty *sonneteer* in his youth.'

'I think you mistake, Mr Palmer. Sonnets, yes, but holy and not in his youth – those were ... other matter.'

Palmer smiled his concession of the point. He had already made his.

He did not escape scot-free. Brother Palmer was loaded with extra duties, more church services to attend than the expected minimum. They restricted his time for what else he had to do. It was some days before he could return to Emilia Lanier's house.

He found the women away. Only Henry Lanier was at home. The man was friendlier than Palmer might have expected given the past.

'Your goddaughter is a good young woman, Mr Palmer.'

Palmer's suspicious ears twitched. Were Emilia's fears well-placed, about a young man and woman under the same roof?

Lanier saw it.

'I have a sweetheart of my own, Mr Palmer, someone I hope will become my wife.'

This news relieved Palmer.

'Does your mother know about her?'

Something told Palmer she might not. Lanier confirmed it.

'Joyce Mansfield is not who my mother might have in mind. She is a draper's daughter.'

'I see, not grand enough perhaps?'

Lanier laughed.

'Perhaps so although to be fair, I believe my mother would understand an alliance among our own kind, among musicians connected with the Court. It is shop-trade her prejudice lies against. In fact, there is a matter on which I'd value your advice....'

Did advice mean help? Palmer asked himself, anxious not to cross Emilia, especially in family matters.

'... on certain matters which need to be negotiated in respect of the marriage....'

Palmer bet they did, including whether a merchant would welcome a musician as a son-in-law.

'... I mean the money arrangements, Joyce's dowry in particular. I have no father, Mr Palmer to whom I can entrust the matter.'

A line crossed Palmer's mind, heard somewhere that it was a wise man who knew his father. Who was the father of the man in front of him? Not his stepfather, in blood or kindness, Alphonso Lanier whose nose Palmer had squashed in revenge for the small matter of trying to kill him on the road from Stratford. As for William Shakespeare, he was dead half a dozen years. The noble Lord Southampton? He was living still, rich as Croesus too. The old Lord Hunsdon, Emilia's first keeper was not, he was long gone down into dust.

Lanier's next question surprised Palmer.

'My father, what was he like? Not my stepfather, my real one.'

Palmer spread his hands. Where to start? He looked the man up and down again convinced by his resemblance to the actor, not to any of the noble lords Emilia would prefer it to be, not spindly old Hunsdon or foxy-featured Southampton.

'Do you want the truth? It is an opinion your mother might not agree with and she ought to know.'

Lanier thought for a moment and then nodded.

Palmer told him who.

'And what was he like, Mr Shakespeare?'

Palmer paused.

'Your height and build, same colour hair....'

'Yes, but what was he *like*?'

Successful at what he did writing the modern drama which Palmer despised for its lack of obedience to the old classical rules and for making trade out of the sacred muse; but then wasn't that how the young man in front of him was earning his living, in his case from music?

'He made a name for himself,' Palmer said, 'he made money, enough to buy one of the biggest houses in his home town and to marry his daughter well, to a *gentleman*.'

Palmer called to mind the good Dr Hall so recently met on the road to Oxford. From Henry's continuing look of expectation, it needed more he could see.

'He was ... a prudent man in the main.'

But not when he became mixed up with treason and traitors including Lanier senior over the small matter of a play to get the mob in the mood for regicide; this Palmer kept quiet about.

'So, he has family.'

'A daughter and granddaughter.'

'Where?'

'Where? It's best you don't know where, there is nothing for you there. Think instead of your Miss ... Mansfield wasn't it?'

'I shall, Mr Palmer. When you help me, by acting as my go-between over the dowry.'

'Now wait a moment....'

~ 5 ~

'Do you know much about the drapery business, Mr Palmer?'

Whether he did or not, the bald draper in front of him was about to tell him.

Palmer weathered a storm of detail, about how drapery had been when the man in front of him had started in business and where it was now, what with the effect of changing fashions or the waves of prosperity, down as well as up and the risks but not the rewards – oh no, the draper was too smart to declare his hand this early in the negotiation over his daughter's dowry!

'My daughter Joyce has told me only so much about young Master Lanier and his family.'

Palmer opened his mouth to explain but he was beaten to it.

'... I understand that he is, or will be a musician at *Court*, in the *royal* service....'

Obviously a plus point to a draper, Palmer calculated.

'... as was his father....'

'*Was*,' Palmer emphasised, 'he died nine years ago with the military rank of captain and in the enjoyment of a royal prerogative.'

'Ah yes, something to do with the weighing of hay?'

'Indeed. He was a valiant soldier,' Palmer lied, who had seen the man's cowardice close to on three occasions, the last when he had flattened his nose. 'He was recruited by my Lords Essex and Southampton in their great campaigns against the Spaniards.'

'Such a pity about the Essexs,' the draper began to say, meaning both of them, the unfortunate father and the unlucky son – the one who had been executed for rebellion against the old Queen, Elizabeth, Palmer's first case – the other, restored to favour under King James whose wife had taken a lover who happened to be the King's boyfriend and capped it all by poisoning an inconvenient go-between.

'... such scandals! But Lord Southampton, now....'

Any draper would happily do business with the Southampton name, that much Palmer could see. He offered the man no encouragement.

'Captain Lanier was, I take it, the stepfather?' Mansfield asked.

Palmer chewed this over.

'Actually the father, in the eye of the Law. He was married to his wife Emilia at the time of the birth.'

The draper chuckled.

'In Law,' he said, 'but not perhaps in fact?'

Was this a bargaining point, Palmer asked himself, a way of reducing the portion to be paid out? Or would a hint of grander origins enhance the price? Palmer plumped for the latter.

'Mrs Lanier was brought up in the household of the Countess of Kent. In consequence the Lord Chamberlain of the day, Lord Hunsdon took her under his protection, orphan as she had become.'

The draper was almost salivating – cousin of the old Queen, her half-brother some said who reckoned his sire to be old King Hal himself. Royal blood, royal blood about to run in Draper Mansfield's family!

'How much?'

The draper's gaze turned shrewd as he asked the question.

Palmer affected nonchalance.

'She will come and live with Mrs Lanier,' he began by saying, 'who wishes to give any children of the union the sort of *noble* education she received herself.'

It had been the only way he could pull Emilia down from the roofbeams when he had broached the subject of the Mansfield marriage and his own role as honest broker.

'Throw himself away on a draper's daughter!' she had shouted.

A wealthy draper's daughter, a good portion to be had, a good trade to draw funds from should anything go wrong with music-making he told her. Palmer remembered how old John Hemmings had funded himself through the bad times for actors by means of his wife's grocery shop.

He hadn't made much headway with Emilia. It took her son to.

'I *will* marry Joyce,' he had told her.

'We shall happily provide all the household effects for the young couple,' the draper said, matching Palmer's offer of a home.

So, how much?

'Two hundred pounds,' Palmer said as if it was a sum of trifling consequence.

It was enough to keep a working man for his entire adult life.

'Two … *two hundred* pounds? However do you come to such a sum?'

The draper appeared genuinely astonished.

Palmer examined his fingernails which were cleaner than he expected. Life in the Charterhouse had certainly improved his physical condition.

'I acted only this year in the case of another family, Oxford people,' he said, looking down his nose to indicate that they could hardly compare with a draper from St Andrew's by-the-Wardrobe in the City of London. 'The girl brought with her exactly that sum.'

'And what was the father's rank in life?'

Palmer imagined John Davenant, astute businessman and Mayor of Oxford turning in his grave.

'Tavern-keeper I believe,' he said, returning his gaze to his fingers.

They settled for one hundred and fifty with no conditions beyond those required by the Law.

Palmer's step was happy as he made his way back to Emilia Lanier's house in Clerkenwell. It faltered and then stopped as he saw the man standing outside it.

'Mr Palmer,' the man said in the accent Palmer could not place except that he was speaking in a second tongue. 'It is midsummer day. You should have come to me in Deptford.'

Palmer hadn't forgotten his debt of twenty-two shillings and sixpence, he simply didn't have it, not even the ten shillings left over after the trip to Oxford. A few necessary expenses and several unnecessary evenings drinking in the Bell Inn had seen to that.

'Let us go inside,' Palmer said.

Emilia and Henry were there, so was Miracle by the sound of her working in the back-kitchen.

Palmer gave the pair the good news about the dowry. Henry smiled broadly, his mother grimaced.

'This is what I have been doing,' he explained to his lender.

And why he did not have the money he felt he did not have to say.

The remaining gold angels for Miracle burned against his breast. He put them out of his mind. They had been his once but they were not his to part with unless it was to Miracle's benefit.

'Business is business,' the man said. 'The money is due.'

'I do not have it.'

The man sighed.

'I presumed not.'

'Then why are you here?'

'Because you were not at your lodgings in the Charterhouse.'

'You have been to the Charterhouse?'

Palmer was aghast.

'Yes, to the Charterhouse. I viewed your security for the debt, your bed and its linen. It is handsome. It will cover the debt.'

It was more than handsome, Palmer wanted to scream, it was all he had left of his past, of what the Palmer name had once meant in the world. Now it was reduced to security for the precise amount of twenty-two shillings and sixpence! He had only himself to blame.

'And what will I sleep on?' he asked, anger in his voice.

'That is your concern, not mine.'

Another voice intervened, Henry Lanier's.

'Zio, you have heard what Mr Palmer has done for me. He has stood in the place of my father, he has acted as family.'

The man looked Lanier up and down.

'He is not of our people. Your wife-to-be, she is not of our people. Business is business. I took the debt because you asked me to. It has cost me money to come here to pursue it.'

Henry Lanier reached inside his clothing.

'Then the debt is mine.'

From a leather purse he counted out two weighty crowns, three half crowns, five smaller shilling pieces and a sixpence, extending them in his open hand. The man counted coin by coin, transferring them to his own purse.

'The debt is paid,' he said, turning on his heel and leaving the house without another word.

'Miracle cannot stay here,' said Emilia, 'not once Henry is married. Children will come. There is little enough room here as it is.'

Problems upon problems. Palmer was not surprised he had never been tempted to be a family man.

'It won't be for a year, Mother.'

The voice was Henry's.

'For a year?'

How much relief and how much surprise was in Emilia's response Palmer found difficult to gauge.

'Joyce and I are agreed. One of the King's musicians is not in best health so I have the chance of his position. Until I do I must work as and when the need arises in place of this man and until he... leaves the King's service. Until then my position is not sure.'

'A lot can happen in a year.'

All three knew what Emilia was saying – sickness, death and dowries unpaid in consequence.

'My Will will come for me, I know he will!'

No-one had noticed Miracle come in from the kitchen.

Will Davenant, sixteen years old and a student with no prospects. It was what Palmer was afraid of. With a bit of luck Miracle was out of his sight and mind and his cock pointing like a lodestone elsewhere.

'We need not think about this until next summer,' Henry said kindly.

Emilia was not quite so kind. She parted Palmer from another gold angel for Miracle's keep.

~ 6 ~

RICHARD FIELD was an unexpected sighting in the street for Palmer, wandering as he was away from his Charterhouse territory early one afternoon. He would have avoided him had they not bumped into each other turning a corner. Field was not alone.

Both men decided on civility.

'This is Mr Richard Palmer, once of the Revels office among *other* things. Mr Palmer, Master Jaggard....'

Another of the inky fraternity Palmer guessed and rightly. They were all men of the same age.

'... Mr Palmer used to try to sell me stale old plays including those by my late lamented friend Will Shakespeare.'

Palmer took the exchange in a different direction.

'Jaggard? Publisher of some sonnets, I seem to remember including a few by the said Shakespeare.'

'A very few,' Field snorted, 'fewer than the claim on the title-page.'

Both publishers laughed at the deception.

'We called it *The Passionate Pilgrim*,' Jaggard admitted. 'It did well, we reprinted it oh, ten years ago.'

'Yes and the authors complained and made you take their names off it!'

Field's accusation did not embarrass his friend.

'That's authors for you! What I say is, the proof-reading's down to them. If it's wrong it's because they get it wrong. Caveat scriptor.'

Field laughed again.

'You believe in the immaculate compositor. You've always been sharp in your practice, Jaggard. What about those plays of Shakespeare you published?'

'Three years back, ten of 'em. Well, I thought, the author's dead – best sort of author to my mind, a dead one – but the actors weren't happy with me. They put the authorities onto me to get a stay of publication in case they could get money for them elsewhere.'

'So you published anyway.'

'And backdated the publication dates – the Lord Chamberlain should have proscribed me more *tightly* let us say.'

Palmer interrupted their trade bonhomie.

'Well, I know they're interested in publishing now.'

'Who?'

'The actors, the King's Men.'

'How do you know?'

'I know old John Hemmings, I saw him not long past. They're talking of a complete works, all the plays, like Ben Jonson's had done apparently.'

'Yes, he has,' Jaggard mused. 'Tell me, I imagine they are well advanced in their plans....'

'I've heard nothing about it, not around the town, not in the Guild,' Field said, 'but then as Mr Palmer knows, I don't touch plays, never have never will.'

Jaggard eyed Palmer up and down.

'Mr Palmer, the actors are unlikely to be friendly to this your humble servant,' and he mimed a bow. 'If you have their ear and you can bring them to me and my son Isaac then we should be most grateful.'

'How grateful? A tithe on what you might pay the actors? One pound per ten?'

'An unusual arrangement, Mr Palmer. Bring them to us and we will consider.'

'The deliverer requires a promise of satisfaction first.'

Jaggard hesitated and then put out his hand.

'As Master Field is our witness,' he said, 'one pound in ten.'

Emilia Lanier was not at all pleased when Palmer came on his next visit to Miracle. He followed her eyes to see why. They indicated another presence in the recesses of the room.

The figure, a young man's figure turned round. It was William Davenant.

'I have left the University, Mr Palmer,' he said.

Palmer swore audibly before his voice returned to reason.

'Then you have found an apprenticeship, a master in the City as your father wished?'

'Business does not suit me. It's been quite enough proving my father's will which is still to be finished with. I continue to believe that my future lies with the Court.'

'Doing what?'

Miracle interrupted.

'Writing poetry and plays. My William writes beautifully, his godfather Shakespeare was....'

'Not his godfather as far as I know, and yes you are correct, Mr Shakespeare *was* not *is*. For what you both have in mind, patronage will be needed. Who are your friends at Court, young Master William, other than the perfumer?'

Davenant opened his mouth as if to begin a torrent of names. Then he shook his head.

'There is one possibility.'

The voice was Emilia's.

Everyone turned towards her.

What could she possibly offer Palmer complained inwardly?

Her connection with the Court had died nearly thirty years ago when her elderly keeper shuffled her off into an arranged marriage due to an inconvenient pregnancy. Her association with a circle of pious literary ladies was also past and done with, women who had in the main eschewed Court life for godly private devotion. Was Emilia romancing at her age? Palmer asked himself. Again?

'The Duchess of Lennox.'

Palmer whistled in surprise. The Duke was Scots and cousin to the King.

'I knew her as Mrs Prannell in the nineties when she was married to a City alderman, from a family which made its money in wine. She was a client of Dr Forman.'

Who wasn't? Palmer wondered.

'Last year she married Lennox, her lover of some years. Rumour has it that the King intends to welcome Lennox into the English nobility with an appropriate Dukedom.'

'A Double Duchess!' exclaimed Davenant in admiration.

'Frank ... she will listen to me.'

The look Emilia gave Palmer gave him pause. Whatever had happened with Forman, that treater of women's infertility, maker of their horoscopes, confidant over their love affairs and taker of his pleasures in lieu, it bound this circle of women together.

Emilia undoubtedly had something on this woman who had risen so high at Court.

'Frank?' he said, raising a bushy eyebrow.

'Her friends call her so, Lennox does too. She is a Howard, a Viscount's daughter before Prannell's new money bought her hand and body. After him she was old Hertford's wife, a Countess. He kept her cut off out in the country.'

'What will you ask her for?'

'A place in her household for a young man of promise.'

'I should like to be a page,' Davenant said, quick to support her idea. 'A man can rise in the service of the nobility, especially one as noble as Lennox and so near the King.'

Emilia refused to have young Davenant in her house. Palmer was forced to send him to his own lodgings in the Charterhouse despite the problems it was bound to create with the Preacher.

He decided to speak to Miracle in private and to complete a duty he had been putting off for weeks. He took her to the Churchyard of St James's. He found the place he was looking for under an old yew tree.

'Your mother Ellen is buried here,' he told her.

'Is it consecrated ground?'

He told her that it was and that the tree might well be older than the church.

'Old wives' tales tell that the people first worshipped around trees such as this.'

'Who did they worship? The God of our Bible and Prayerbook?'

'Who can say? Any power they saw as greater than themselves more like.'

'Sun, moon and stars?'

'Savages in the new world do the same, or so we read. In classical times there were many gods, one even for a little place such as this. They called it genius loci, the spirit of the place.'

'The nymph of the river or the glade?'

'Sometimes, yes.'

They stood in silence. Palmer could see that Miracle was praying.

When she was ready he told her as much as was seemly about Ellen's death – finding softer ways to describe her place in the bawdy house, her being with child, the bawd kicking her to death.

'He's dead now I'm pretty sure.'

'May God have mercy on his soul.'

As she said it, Miracle turned full face towards him.

'Am I like her, must I be like her?'

Palmer took her hands, not something he was used to doing with young women or any women.

'You have a lot of her in your figure and face. You have more of your foster-mother Jane in your character. Some take this as an unkind saying but your mother was no better than she should be. Fate dealt her a difficult lot, it swallowed her up.'

'Some might say the same about me.'

Palmer paused for thought.

'My father now, he was unshakeable in his faith, the old faith – he was a recusant, he refused to conform. I am not he, that's my point.'

'What happened to him?'

'He died a disappointed man. We lost everything.'

'I have William,' Miracle said. 'I know what you think, that he's a young man with a young man's intentions not to be relied on....'

'I have been a young man myself.'

Briefly, he admitted to himself, thinking back to Kentish days and the failed courtship of a young Emilia Bassano who'd had grander, more ambitious notions than to be Mrs Palmer.

'... but I've known him for ever, we have been as one all our lives.'

Palmer dropped his hands away from hers.

'Then we must do things properly. Let him get himself a situation to support a wife and the children who will follow. There is money in his father's will for him but it cannot replace gainful employment. If he does this let us call the banns and stand you both up in front of the people in church. And Miracle, get to the altar before you go to his bed....'

Miracle laughed mischievously.

'You're too late there Uncle Two Names.'

It was a short walk from Clerkenwell across the noisy Farringdon Road towards Ely House in Holborn.

'What am I to expect of the Duchess, Mrs Prannell as was?'

Palmer asked his question as he and Emilia were trudging through mud and worse, avoiding horses and carts and the rougher sorts of humankind on their way to wherever they were going.

'I haven't seen her in more than twenty years.'

'Not since the Forman days?'

Emilia gave him a sharp look.

'Frank was always very beautiful. When she married crusty old Hertford one of her admirers cut his own throat.'

'Whyever did he do that?'

'He'd written some nonsense about dying for love, she wrote back that no-one ever did so he decided to prove her wrong!'

More fool he.

'You sound as if you knew her well.'

A silence fell between them until Emilia decided to speak.

'While she was married to Prannell – ten years in all, before he died – she fell in love....'

Palmer was not sure he wanted to listen to female stories of romance. He'd had years of following the Alderman's wife and romance was not what he had witnessed. Pumping arses and splayed thighs was not Lancelot and Guinevere. On second thoughts....

'... in love with Henry Wriothesley, Lord Southampton....'

Palmer stopped in his muddy tracks.

He was all ears. So the two women were sisters in love with foxy young Southampton? Emilia had been there first, before Frances, amid a whirl of sonnets which had turned into a blizzard of recrimination as a poet lost his lady to the young man who was his patron, and felt the patron's loss the more. Shakespeare, Emilia, and Southampton, Palmer's first case when Shakespeare was in trouble.

'Did you talk about him together?'

'Heavens no! I heard it from Forman – he could be very indiscreet when he wanted to provoke me. What I told him about Southampton I suspect he told her. When I met her once or twice she looked at me as if she knew, as if we each carried a cross, the same cross.'

Whatever it was it eluded Palmer, this effect of Southampton on women. Was it that he never pursued them, leaving them to chase him?

He concentrated instead on what they were about to try to achieve. Emilia had written to the Duchess who sent word back stating time and place – so far so good. The boy Davenant had been sent off to a good tailor to buy clothes fit for a young gentleman hoping for a place in a noble household from the forty pounds specifically provided in his father's will to equip him for a business career. This *was* a kind of business, Emilia said. Twice as much as was needed came back with him from the tailor, of a quality fit for a lord not a page. The boy had extravagant tastes, a warning to Palmer but not to Miracle who was full of admiration for her kitted-up beau.

Davenant was not to accompany his go-betweens today.

'I must place the idea first with Her Grace and then the boy can go in and win her over. Frank likes a good-looking face and young Davenant has that. As for you,

Richard – you're the respectable gentleman-pensioner, mind, and his godfather....'

'... which I'm not, I'm Miracle's.'

'We must stretch a point in this case.'

They made their way to the porter's lodge at Ely House. The porter sent a boy who returned with a gentleman servitor who took them to the steward of the household, a middle-aged man with a head which reminded Palmer of a badger's.

They progressed from room to room each one smaller than the one before, more richly panelled and more decorated with wood carvings and portraits of the better, Flemish sort in matching browns, blacks and whites. Everywhere members of the household were busy about their business in an entourage not much short of regal in number. The Double Duchess-to-be lived in style.

At the last room, Palmer held back while Emilia was introduced into the sanctum sanctorum, what he understood to be Her Grace's closet, her private room for business and meeting friends.

It was some time before anyone came out.

The first person who did was the Duchess. She was a round-faced woman bisected by an aquiline nose eased by an amiable smile; her middle height owed much to hair swept back straight and piled unnaturally high. How much of it was real in substance or in its red-blonde colour? An eerie thought came to Palmer, that what she and her one-time rumoured lover Southampton would have seen in each other was ... themselves. He did not have an eye for the detail of her dress beyond a guess that the fabric of her clothes and the quality of her ropes of pearls cost more than he had earned in a lifetime.

'So you, Mr Palmer are the godfather of young Master de Avenant.'

Half surprised by her pronunciation Palmer could barely shape his lips into a rictus of agreement before the Duchess was onto her next question.

'I am told by dearest Mrs Lanier here that he was educated at the University, in Oxford....

Palmer maintained the awkward rictus.

'... and that his father did service to the State, as Mayor of that city.'

Palmer's lips were getting tired with smiling.

'And the father was a vinter too. Fancy that – it was the trade of my first husband's family, Mr Prannell.'

Her voice picked up pace.

'Now, what would you say this young gentleman's personal qualities are – in respect of a page's position in this household. I ask from a man's point of view. I must think of my husband the Duke above myself.'

Palmer didn't believe her for a moment but he had already been tutored to present the boy's masculine qualities in ways that would please a woman.

'He has all the required skills and education of a gentleman. He can sing, play and paint a little I believe but more than these, he is accomplished in writing, whether it be in verse or in prose.'

The Duchess had herself written for the public eye and with some wit, Emilia had told him who had appeared in print herself, in her case on the less witty subject of religion. If it sounded odd coming as a recommendation from his own lips he could see at once the welcome effect it was having on the Duchess, his preaching to the only-too-ready to be converted.

Palmer played the trump card Emilia had instructed.

'I should tell Your Grace that Mr William Shakespeare was a familiar of the, er, de Avenant family both in Oxford and earlier in London.'

The Duchess clapped her hands like a young girl which she no longer was. Palmer put her in her forties, the bloom a touch dry but by no means blown.

'We *adore* the plays of Mr Shakespeare! They are still wanted at Court where the King's Men remain much in demand. We have the actors from time to time here in Ely House.'

Palmer was not surprised.

The Duchess made a decision.

'Young Mr de Avenant should present himself here … let us say tomorrow around ten in the morning, before my husband goes out. Let us see what my husband makes of him.'

'Well then, how did it go?'

Miracle was asking her young swain, dressed in his expensive best new suit in Emilia Lanier's house after his return from his interview with the Duke and the Duchess.

Davenant was too excited to come to the point. He had a story and he was determined to tell it in all its glory in his own time.

'Her Grace was as I was told she would be, affable, condescending but not above showing her quality, example, all manner of names she spouted – the King, the Prince, Duke this, Earl that … I corrected her on one point.'

'And what was that?'

Palmer hoped the boy hadn't ruined his chances by acting too smart.

'She called me de Avenant. I said that was wrong.'

Emilia who had invented the curlicue, looked annoyed.

'It's all right,' the boy said, 'I told her it was D apostrophe.'

He pronounced the name in the French style, 'D'Avenon.'

'I'm sure it was once upon a time!'

'What about *His* Grace?' Palmer pressed him.

'I liked him, he has a sense of humour and he stands no nonsense from the Duchess. When she was busy dropping names he said….'

Davenant took up an actor's position, of a middle-aged courtier.

'… Frank,' – it's true it's what he calls her – 'Frank, how long ago was it when you were plain Mrs Prannell?'

Emilia laughed out loud.

'And how did *she* take it?'

'With good *grace*,' Davenant punned. 'In short, I am to be a page in the Lennox household!'

Miracle flung her arms around him.

'Then we can be married!'

Davenant pushed her away affectionately.

'Let me settle into the position first.'

When he saw her disappointment he quickly added, 'What could be better? I shall be in Ely House in sight of you and you in sight of me.'

'The boy is right,' Emilia said. 'Miracle, understand this, a woman of position of whatever age likes to feel that she still commands the *devotion* of her men and her menservants. The Duchess must feel that young William here is hers. It doesn't mean what you think – at least it shouldn't and I know Frank to be a woman of sense in these things, ever since she rejoined the nobility.'

'I do understand,' Miracle said. 'It is a game such people play.'

Palmer received no goodwill from the Preacher in the Charterhouse.

'Mr Palmer, Mr Palmer, always Mr Palmer, what are we to do with you?'

Palmer stayed silent. The Preacher tried again.

'I understand that you have been accommodating a young man in your lodgings. This is strictly against our rules. No doubt you are going to tell me that he is your ... nephew?'

A glint in the cleric's eyes showed what he was implying. Palmer wasn't having it.

'He is my godson. He was orphaned in the spring – both his parents within weeks of each other. In consequence he has taken leave from his studies at the University in Oxford and is to be a page to His Grace the

Duke of Lennox over the way in Ely House. He will be leaving my lodgings forthwith.'

Game, set and match Palmer reckoned.

'His Grace you say? Well, that does make a difference ... although you might have, em, had a word, with me first?'

Palmer nodded gruffly.

'As for His Grace, *Their* Graces, I do hope that they might one Sunday attend our modest Chapel to hear one of the, em, improving sermons I am most sensible of giving not only to our brethren and our little community here but also to the great and the good, as indeed Their Graces most signally are....'

~ 7 ~

S UMMER GAVE WAY to autumn.

Soon Henry Lanier was reporting on plans for the Christmas season of entertainments at Court in which he was contracted to perform.

'The great change will be working in the new Banqueting Hall in Whitehall.'

Palmer remembered the old one, a stiff, painted tent, cold and inhospitable.

'It is the work of Master Inigo Jones. He builds in the style of the Italian architect Signor Palladio.'

Laddy-o Palladio meant nothing to Palmer.

Work had been going on for the best part of three years, that much Palmer did know who had from time to time gone to see the great stone double cube raise itself in the heart of the old palace like a bright new star installed out of place in an older, duller firmament. Inigo Jones he knew of but had never met, not even when his path had crossed with Jones's masque-writing partner Ben Jonson in the difficult days of the Gunpowder Treason early in the King's reign.

Jones and Jonson had done well from the royal gravy train, that much Palmer knew too. The architect was now Surveyor-General – he was finally getting to build some of those pretty models of his. Jonson was doing as Jonson always did. Hadn't he picked up yet more royal crumbs by purchasing the reversion of the Mastership of the Revels? It amused Palmer to think of Jonson, perennial trouble to the Censor one day turning Censor himself and putting on all the Court entertainments. Pity the rival playwrights who applied to him!

'There's bound to be a masque,' he grumbled, mindful of muscle memories of an arse-numbing version by the same team all those years ago extolling the virtues of marriage.

Henry Lanier laughed.

'There certainly is. It is to be called *Time vindicated to himself and to his honours.*'

'Says it all,' said Palmer.

'I know nothing about it other than this – I will be among the parley of musicians as opposed to a quarrel of actors or a fidget of dancers....'

That did say it all, to Palmer's mind.

'... and the masquers will be led in the dance by none other than His Royal Highness, Prince Charles.'

Palmer realised the significance – Lanier's hopes of confirmation of a Court position were closely tied to the royal Prince and Heir to the Throne.

'So they'll have to surround him with dwarves!'

Palmer was picking on the Prince's tiny stature, less than five and a half feet tall.

Charles was a second son, the eldest Henry, every inch what a prince should be having died of fever ten years before. What sort of a king Charles might make nobody knew. From what Lanier said the Prince was most at home with books, music, plays and paintings. His greatest task – other than dancing in this masque – was to make a royal marriage. The favourite bride in prospect, old King James's favourite, that is, was a Spanish one, Maria Anna. With a bit of luck the royal Infanta was smaller than the Prince.

It was only because Miracle wanted to go that Palmer, with heavy heart and heavier feet accepted Lanier's offer of free entry to the spectacle.

'William will be there,' Miracle urged her godfather, 'in the Lennox train.'

And he was too, seated in one of the lowest positions according to his page's rank among the thousand and more packed into the main hall. Miracle waved at him from their place in the gallery reached by an external staircase which accommodated the other classes, the unwashed ones as Palmer could smell around him, like the groundlings in the public playhouses. He saw Davenant smile back.

Palmer found the storyline as Jonsonianly obscure as ever. Fame entered accompanied by a trio called the Curious Three who were just that, each sporting an eye, ear or nose but not all three. The set was a panorama of the palace itself, pride of place given to, what else, the image of the new banqueting house! Dramatic exchanges rolled out obsessed with the political scandal of the day.

'Why can't he leave satire alone?' Palmer said to no-one in particular as disapproving rumblings in the audience greeted what was being acted on stage.

When the Curious Three carried a whip-cracking Satyr off, it was not before time.

'Oh look!'

Miracle pointed to the main business of the masque at last getting underway; Saturn and Venus processed in with their acolytes followed by Cupid and Diana.

'Be careful what you wish for.'

As if in answer to Palmer's warning the much-advertised noble masquers, amateur gentlemen of the Court revealed themselves in a dancing troupe led by

Prince Charles. The music struck up a livelier beat in response, Henry Lanier attacking his viol in the heart of the consort of musicians.

'A coranto!' Miracle exclaimed, 'and now a galliard!'

Palmer had never been much of a dancer, least of all the peculiar step of the galliard – short bursts of steps in contrasting rhythms accompanied by music sounded in a succession of clashing pitches. It looked as if the dancers were trying to run before they could walk!

He could only admire the tiny Prince as he executed weightless leaps held a little longer in the air than the accompanying beat. Once landed he brought his feet quickly back into time – he didn't miss a step which couldn't be said for some of the others around him. The Prince *was* tiny, an almost feminine figure with his long well-shaped hair in the modern fashion, a youthful beard trimmed narrowly around the mask of the face. There was a look of blithe serenity over intense concentration as if this act of self-display meant everything, here today and in life in front of these, the right people.

Only one dancer bettered him, older, more athletic and of obvious interest to the husk of the King who sat alone out front – his wife dead these last three years and separated from him for the previous dozen. Old James was hunched on his royal throne opposite the stage gazing at his 'Steenie', his 'wifey', his greatest ever favourite and Chief Minister in all but name, George Villiers Marquess of Buckingham.

'The Marquess dances best.'

The voice, thin and aged, froze Palmer to the spot. He turned to see an ancient wraith in patched clothes. He knew he knew him but where from? His mind returned to the days of his best client, Robert Cecil, Villiers's political predecessor. It was his old paymaster, that's who it was, Cecil's official who had disappeared on the death of his master ten years ago. Palmer did not ask him how he was – his evident poverty spoke the answer.

'When Villiers is made Duke – and he must be soon – His Grace as he will become shall be entitled to dance alongside His Royal Highness rather than behind him.'

Title and order; Palmer smiled at the old man's perennial fascination. He guessed at his situation – a small quarterly pension of shillings and pennies irregularly paid, a bed somewhere below the social surface unconnected with the new religion, more likely with the old. From time to time he would come out to observe great occasions like this evening's, from the fringes.

'We have seen the best, yes we have seen the best....'

The frail old man was turning to slip out ahead of time.

Palmer put his hand on the man's tattered sleeve struggling to find the flesh within it. At the same time he reached inside his own clothes. He had one golden angel left. He owed it to Emilia for Miracle's care. There would be arguments....

He slipped the coin into the old man's hand which closed like a claw around it.

'God grant you grace,' the man said vanishing towards the exit staircase.

Out front at last the spectacle was over, to relieved applause.

'We are to meet Henry behind the scenes,' Miracle said. 'William will meet us there too.'

Ben Jonson was holding forth to a small circle.

'Master Jones can say what he likes but a spectacle does not exist without a story, or a story without words, scenes, drama, dialogue and, yes, the resonating muse of music. As far as I know nobody comes to the masque just to see the stage design.'

Palmer's eye caught his causing the playwright to pause in his diatribe while he shook off this face from the past.

'As for objections to the satire within the piece....'

Palmer left Jonson's explanation behind him.

He saw that Miracle had found her William.

William was enthusiastic.

'I should like to try my hand at the masque,' he announced to Palmer. 'Perhaps I might talk to Mr Jonson. Do you know him, could you introduce me?'

'I do, but he's not a man to help anyone other than himself.'

'Then what is my way forward?'

The new Master of the Revels, Palmer supposed, but why should he listen to some callow neophyte, yet another young hopeful who thought he could write.

He caught sight of a couple of faces in the crowd he recognised, actors, John Hemmings and another veteran he couldn't put a name to. It would make sense for them to be there, senior King's Men overseeing the professional actors employed in the masque. They might be a way forward for an aspiring writer. Was it what he should be encouraging Davenant towards? What good would it do Miracle?

Palmer shrugged his shoulders and excused himself, aiming for the actors.

Hemmings tried to avoid his glance. Unforewarned the other actor was friendlier.

'Henry Condell,' he said when Palmer extended his hand.

'Are you still looking to publish the works of your late colleague Shakespeare?'

A look of surprise passed over Condell's face.

'Yes, well, yes, we've talked about it, haven't we, John?'

Hemmings turned back, a look of pained politeness on his face.

'Who would you choose to publish it?'

'It's not as simple as that, Mr Palmer,' Hemmings said smoothly. 'First we have to establish the true list of the author's works....'

'... taking into account those written by himself alone, the collaborations and the works which antedate our company and their ownership in Law,' Condell explained.

'Then we have to gather together the prompt books....'

'... and look at his original papers where the performing editions are not everything he wrote – *Hamlet* for example is half the length in performance of what he actually set down.'

Palmer cut to the kill.

'Who wouldn't you work with among the publishers?'

'Ha!' The stage laugh was Hemmings's. 'They're all rogues!'

'Some more than others,' Condell remonstrated mildly with him.

Business was business.

'Assuming the publisher was reputable, what price would you take?'

Hemmings's eyes tuned beadier.

'Mr Palmer, if the publisher is reputable, and will pay, oh, one hundred pounds....'

The sum was intended to shock.

'How many plays are we talking about?' Palmer asked.

Condell reflected.

'Somewhere between thirty and forty.'

'A good discount per play,' Palmer said, remembering the old rate for plays published in his brief time in the office of the Master of the Revels – five or six pounds each.

'When you have an offer of one hundred pounds then we shall talk, Mr Palmer. Henry?'

The actors executed a perfect exit.

'A hundred pounds?'

William Jaggard was appalled.

Palmer switched his pitch towards Jaggard's son Isaac in their printing works in the Barbican in the heart of the old City.

'Could Shakespeare's collected works sell for a pound? I've seen individual plays sell for anything from sixpence to a shilling per copy. Is there no premium for a full collection?'

The son appeared to be giving it more thought.

'That would mean selling one hundred copies of the Folio.'

'One hundred and ten,' Palmer checked him, 'including what your father agreed to pay me.'

'You forget the costs of production,' William Jaggard added, 'the materials, wages, ink, the commission for the booksellers....'

His son came to a figure.

'So it's a risk of two hundred pounds, say. Two hundred copies before we're in profit.'

'Jaggard? The *Jaggards*?'

John Hemmings was not impressed, standing in the penthouse above the stage in the Globe playhouse where Palmer had arranged to bring the prospective publishers.

Condell, Palmer noted looked calmer.

They heard steps on wooden stairs approaching from below.

'That will be Isaac,' Palmer said, 'Jaggard the son.'

His choice had been deliberate, off with the old, William who had given the actors offence more than once in the past, look to the future, Isaac.

Isaac Jaggard was crisp in his presentation.

'We would produce the works in Folio size – that's eight and a half by thirteen and three quarters – inches that is – single-fold printed in sixes on the best linen paper – we're allowing up to one thousand leaves per folio....'

Palmer whistled. It was a library in itself. How many words might a man produce if he did nothing else in life but scribble?

'... buckram covers for those as want them or bound according to the customer's instructions.'

'And the typeface?'

The practical question was Condell's.

'Roman, our own version – we will apply five compositors to setting it. We believe it would make sense to divide the plays up into sections – comedies, histories, tragedies....'

'What about tragi-comical histories?'

Condell's in-joke was lost on the young publisher who ploughed on regardless.

'... and we need to select the best and most popular play to front the book. What the customer sees first will decide him.'

Palmer was keeping his eyes on the actors' faces. From what he saw a deal could be on.

Hemmings had a question.

'And what do you suppose that leading play should be? *Richard III, Romeo & Juliet, Julius Caesar*? I played important parts in all three. My Montague....'

Jaggard quickly cut him off.

'We must look to the most spectacular, a proven favourite at Court or in the Blackfriars Theatre – that's where our market is at one pound a pop, the quality market with the money.'

Condell was sanguine.

'*The Tempest*, you must mean.'

Isaac Jaggard considered it before nodding approvingly. It was what he had wanted all along.

'We both played in *Tempest*, didn't we John?' said Condell, smoothing the path.

'So that's settled,' Jaggard said quickly. 'We will need a top class dedication to the high and mighty.'

'We've thought about that already....'

'... the Herbert brothers.'

Jaggard whistled, impressed.

'The Lord Chamberlain and his brother and heir, who could be better?'

This office of State held supreme authority over the plays and players.

'Only George Villiers,' Condell laughed.

'And other dedications in support, high-placed friends of the late author in prose, in verse....'

'In Latin *and* Greek?'

The joke came from Condell.

Hemmings grumbled.

'Not if we don't want to upset Ben Jonson.'

'Jonson sells,' Jaggard said. 'His own collected works have.'

'And him still a *living* author,' Hemmings sneered before changing his tone.' Maybe *he* would do it, write something in honour of the man who gave him his first chance?'

Jaggard looked from one actor to the other.

'Would payment help?'

'It usually does with Ben.'

'I need an image of the author.'

Hemmings rubbed his chin.

'Not as easy as you might think. There's a painted portrait or two in private hands as far as I recall.'

'I could get an engraving done from them.'

'Difficult, difficult. What do you think, Henry?'

'The family? Don't they have a miniature? It might give a resemblance for an engraving.'

'I know a young engraver who can do miracles from the simplest images.'

Cheap too, Jaggard didn't say.

Condell moved the discussion on.

'Assuming we come to agreement, what about the matter of payment to *us*, to the King's Men?'

Jaggard reached into his clothing, pulling out a sheet of paper.

'It's here,' he said, 'a note to our goldsmith asking him to pay the bearer fifty pounds....'

'Fifty pounds!'

Hemmings was outraged.

Jaggard went on as if there were no objection.

'Fifty pounds upfront, fifty more on your delivery of, and our satisfaction with the playscripts. How many are there?'

'Thirty-six,' Condell said. 'Ready and waiting.'

'And scarcely a blot in the handwriting,' Hemmings said. 'Should make it easier for your compositors.'

'Wasn't Master Shakespeare once a scrivener, a professional copyist?'

Hemmings, once a grocer's apprentice, gave Palmer's interruption his severest look.

'Are there any missing?' Jaggard asked.

Both actors passed the question off.

'There's a *King John* we can't lay our hands on....'

'And we don't rate *Pericles* unless as a rescue play. It was mainly the work of George Wilkins.'

Palmer kept his mouth shut – he knew Wilkins. He was the murderer of Miracle's mother in his bawdy house in Clerkenwell. Palmer had fixed him for sure. He sensed that the actors had no brief for him either. Wilkins was to be brushed away into nonentity.

'Do we have a deal?'

Jaggard was showing anxiety for the first time.

Hemmings looked at Condell.

Condell nodded. Hemmings extended his hand to the young publisher.

'... with one condition.'

'And that is?'

'A list of the *principal* actors in Shakespeare's plays. We must feature prominently towards the front of the book. Don't you agree, Henry? The reader would expect it.'

Condell gave his second consent.

Palmer's payment from Jaggard came in gold, five single pound pieces with five yet to come on completion of the job.

The transfer was made in the relative quiet and safety of the back room in the Bell Inn, Carter Lane over a couple of tankards of beer. For Palmer it brought back memories of better times.

He had stayed on briefly with the actors at the Globe, long enough to hear something which meant nothing to him at the time.

'We really ought to rescue Will's bust from Dutch Johnson or Janssen or whatever he calls himself,' Condell had said to Hemmings as Palmer was tackling the steep wooden stairs down from the penthouse. 'The good Dr Hall in Stratford ought to pay.'

~ 8 ~

THE YEAR BROUGHT Villiers his Dukedom.

It also brought him an escapade with the Prince of Wales, both travelling incognito to Madrid in romantic pursuit of the Infanta of Spain. It failed badly over the small matters of religion and decorum. The match was called off. The humiliated Prince was once again in search of a wife.

'They say he will now look towards France and its Princesses.'

Emilia Lanier's informant was the young Lennox page, William Davenant. From a place by the fire Palmer looked on but barely listened, his mind elsewhere.

It had been a satisfactory year for him. The second payment from Jaggard was safely received as were all the Shakespeare playscripts, so the publisher had told Palmer who was less interested in this than in the remaining five gold pieces due to him, promptly handed over. From it he paid Emilia for Miracle's keep and repaid Henry Lanier the twenty-two shillings and sixpence debt to the Deptford chandler. It left him handsomely in funds. The Bell Inn was seeing more of him than for some years.

Left alone with the boy Davenant, Palmer took his chance.

'How is life in the Lennox household?'

'Richmond & Lennox,' the page corrected him, the Duke having been introduced into the English nobility.

Palmer detected a hint of caution.

'Are you getting on?'

Both men knew why he was asking, because of Miracle.

'I am doing my duties. I *have* helped with some of the household entertainments, the writing, performing and staging.'

One aspect of his writing was giving him trouble, praise of his patrons the Duke and Duchess. The Duke couldn't care less, that much he knew, but Her Grace now, she was a different matter. Her Grace expected, just what he had already found out.

'My Lady wishes to see you in her chamber.'

In her chamber? The hour was late, the Duke was out carousing and would spend the night in his grace-and-favour apartment in the Palace of Whitehall. The servants were mostly off duty except for this, the Duchess's personal maid.

Davenant had riffled desperately among his papers looking for a half-begun verse which might satisfy My Lady. The theme he wanted was one of noble couples but every single one he thought of had a flaw. Granted the pair had been lovers before they were man and wife so he had some latitude yet all the stories he could think of ended badly. Dido and Aeneas – desertion and suicide; Theseus and his Amazon Queen – marriage by conquest in war; Abelard and Heloise – Davenant crossed his legs at the thought of the monk's fate. Hero and Leander – the Lennoxs were a bit old for that and he didn't see the Duke flattered to be the Hellespont-swimming foolhardy youth. Was there matter in Ariadne on Naxos with the god Bacchus? No, the Duchess's first husband had been in the wine business, the Duke might not appreciate the allusion.

In growing despair he had thought of borrowing elsewhere from Shakespeare or Donne, but no, it wouldn't work, the Duchess was too well read.

He was led unarmed and resigned into his mistress's chamber. He heard the maid retire behind him, the door close. Was it the lock turning?

The Duchess lay propped up in bed in her nightshift – Huguenot lacework but a nightshift all the same. Cut low it revealed impressive firm white breasts but then all her dresses did, they were her finest feature. Her hair fell undressed and red-blonde around her shoulders lightening a little heaviness in her face tending to a double chin. Pouting lips were emphasised by rouge. She presented an artful vision of the taste of previous reign, a plump Elizabethan Cynthia.

Davenant made a mental note: 'Cynthia.'

'I am finding it difficult to find the right subject fit to praise Your Graces....'

'Our Graces? You are too formal Master D'Avenant....'

The Duchess's smile showed off excellent tiny teeth.

'Grace is what comes to me when I think of Your Grace.'

What would *she* say next?

'You are a mature young man, Will, elegant, fine-limbed. Come sit by me.'

He stepped forward to do as he was bid.

'Will your subject, when you find it, be Love?'

Davenant smiled, saying nothing.

'I see it will. Will that be Agape or Eros?'

'I am too young, My Lady to distinguish.'

The Duchess laughed, looking down into his lap and reaching out her hand towards it.

'I see how it stands with you!'

Memory of the encounter was making Davenant feel pleasantly uncomfortable during his interview with Palmer.

'And your money prospects?'

Palmer's question brought him back into the present. The man had avoided matrimony and here he was pursuing one for Miracle. But then as Davenant knew, he was acting as her guardian; women needed marriage for their own and their children's protection. Palmer was only thinking as any godfather would.

Davenant laughed.

'Pages are paid, if pay is the word, no more than our livery, board and lodging and the occasional gift. On the other hand, the writing profession....'

'... is notoriously risky. Writers are on their own, they have no regular stipend.'

'It works for Master Jonson, it worked for William Shakespeare my....'

'Your nothing! They are the exceptions which prove, that is which test the rule. Jonson as we know has cornered the market in masques because he sees too little reward in the public theatre.'

'I can write masque stories *and* verse. I have begun to try my hand already.'

Palmer cut him short.

'Masques are a fashion and fashion changes. You cannot marry a wife on....'

Mistake, and he knew it.

'Exactly, Mr Palmer, what can I marry Miracle on?'

'Is it true you have a girl?'

The Duchess was teasing Davenant after their eros-making. He had judged it best not to answer her.

'Is she your doxy? No, leman would be kinder. Or your betrothed? '

'We have an understanding.'

'Oh sweet, sweet, has there been a hand-fasting?'

He had shaken his head, hearing the cock crow and feeling his own stir.

'And how do we compare, she and I?'

Dangerous ground. He had risked it.

'How do I compare a snowdrop with a damask rose?'

She smelled gorgeously like one too, from its distilled perfume. Miracle smelled only of spring.

'Are you loyal to her?'

Plainly not.

'In my fashion....'

'It is the fashion to be disloyal. Was I loyal to my first husband, poor Mr P? Or to my second? I doubt the Duke is loyal to me. Matters with him stand ... differently to how they did when Eros was our star.'

'Love has its own laws, My Lady....'

In the small Clerkenwell house man and boy looked at each other, wearily in Palmer's case.

'I cannot marry Miracle as a page nor according to you as a writer.'

Davenant's argument was too arch for Palmer's liking.

'There are two things which you forget. The first is your inheritance. You proved the will last autumn, you were left one hundred and fifty pounds.'

'But my bills! Master Urswick my tailor does not come cheap and a man about town must spend on what he wears, where he goes, who he eats with. A man of fashion really has no choice in the matter.'

The boy looked pleased with himself.

Palmer growled.

'You have run ahead of the altar, Miracle has told me so herself if not in so many words. What you spoil Master Davenant, you own.'

The boy's head drooped and then revived.

'And would I make her happy, a poor page, a would-be writer, a ... spendthrift?'

No, Palmer knew he wouldn't. He let the subject drop.

Davenant wasn't finished.

'I am not .... sure about my future in the Richmond & Lennox household.'

What was this? What was he suggesting?

'Oh, the Duke is perfectly happy with me even if he sees me as the Duchess's lapdog.'

'Are you?'

Davenant leaned forward confidentially.

'Not as she would like,' he lied.

Palmer looked the boy over. The Duchess was still a handsome woman and well-placed at Court. She could do a lot for a young man on the make like the boy in front of him.

Davenant might have thought the same had the Duchess not warned him off. He was not to try to take advantage of her. 'My bed is one thing, my reputation in the world quite another.'

'I *do* love Miracle, Mr Palmer, if only love were enough.'

Palmer chewed the revelation over, unsurprised. What would he have done in the boy's situation?

'The actors owe me no favours,' he said at last, 'Jonson neither. I can't help you forward.'

Davenant masked his disappointment.

'What about the Shakespeare connection? His plays live on, they are shortly to be published again as a result of your efforts, his name will once again have currency in the market of informed opinion and patronage and I...'

'... have already had your ears boxed by me for making light of your mother's reputation!'

The boy sighed.

'It is not my imagination alone. Others suggested it before I ever thought it. And as for my mother....'

'What about her?'

'When I asked her outright, she did not deny it.'

The two men sat watching each other in the summer light bleeding into the room from outside. Why did it matter? Palmer asked himself. It was the way of the world. Jane Davenant was not required to be a saint, was she? Shakespeare possessed much laconic Master Davenant didn't.

'By the way, our actors have gone on tour into the country,' Davenant said. 'I am told that this will include Stratford. There's some gossip about a bust of my ... of the late author being set up in the local church – London work, a Dutch master, none of your provincial pottery.'

A last visit to Stratford? Palmer asked himself.

'And your duties here in Ely House?'

'The Duke and Duchess are in the country. My services are in the meantime *dispensable....*'

The Duchess had teased him with that very word after they had together dispensed some more of the medicine which pleased her.

'... so I have been granted leave to spend more time with my family.'

Palmer doubted if he could say the same to the Preacher but the gold coins in his pocket gave him the confidence to chance it.

The ride to Stratford through the last colours of summer was uneventful. Palmer's body protested, the younger man's thrived under the hard riding regime. They lodged at the Bear just over the causeway into the town – Palmer had old history including a violent altercation and an unpaid bill at the Swan opposite. It was more than twenty years ago, would anyone remember?

Davenant's parting from Miracle had been affecting, even Palmer thought so who had a keen nose for play-acting of any kind.

'We go to find the King's Men,' the boy told the girl, saying nothing about the Shakespeare connection.

Palmer exchanged looks with Emilia Lanier, looks experienced in the ways of the world.

Miracle gave William food for the journey and a handkerchief embroidered by her. What was it about handkerchiefs, Palmer asked himself, in the economy of lovers? He had once sat through a play based on the theft of one as a flimsy pretext for world-shaking mayhem.

Stratford was little changed to Palmer's eyes. Similar-looking people appeared to be playing the same old roles. Well, they would be, wouldn't they? They were likely the sons and daughters in facsimile.

He made discreet enquiries which he reported back to young Davenant.

'We've missed Widow Shakespeare, she died a few weeks ago; she lies buried in the church.'

Palmer had pretty much missed her twenty years ago as well, a silent, heavy spirit who kept herself to herself in some sort of private grief.

Davenant looked mildly crestfallen.

'Cheer up, lad – we weren't about to ask her whether you were her husband's byblow!'

The boy laughed.

'The family home – New Place, it's called – is still in the hands of the family.'

'And who are they?'

'The good Dr Hall and his wife, Mrs Susanna, Shakespeare as was.'

Palmer remembered her well, a smart young woman trying to play older than her years in managing the household in her father's absence. It might help that he'd had a friendly enough encounter with the good Doctor on the road not so long ago.

'There's another daughter but she's not talked about much – made a bad marriage, to a wineshopkeeper.'

'Well, I have something in common there given my father Davenant's business!'

'Oh, and the actors are in town....'

They found them easily enough.

It was in the chancel of the church on the edge of town by the river. It took Palmer a small coin to gain entrance from the sexton since the east end of the building was closed off; all to do, Palmer's practised eye could tell with the moving of the altar to under the crossing in the building so that the sacrament could be celebrated in full view of the people in the nave. Once it was the priest's secret.

Such is the fawning on the people in the new religion, he heard his father snort from wherever the old Papist was now.

'Gentlemen, I heard you would be here,' Palmer said cheerfully, approaching a group admiring the funerary monuments on the wall.

He had recognised Hemmings and Condell among a gaggle of, in the main younger actors, the sort the older men sent out on tour. He saw Dr Hall there too and beside him two women, one approaching middle-age, the other between child – her face and figure – and woman – her dress.

Knowing unwelcome when he saw it Palmer smartly introduced his good-looking young companion. Davenant was quick to ingratiate himself among the actors.

'How is your Latin, Mr Palmer?' Dr Hall said, detaching himself from his wife and child to speak to the newcomer.

As good as yours, Palmer wanted to say but held his tongue.

Hall waved his hand in the direction of a plaque on the wall, newly set up from what Palmer could see. He scanned it quickly, the references to the late Mrs Shakespeare, to a mother who had given life and milk. And was that all to be said of her and of a life lived long, sixty-seven years as the inscription inferred?

'Would Mrs Shakespeare have understood it?'

'It is for posterity Mr Palmer rather than for the departed. Perhaps you will approve of this one?'

He guided Palmer's eyes to a bust with an inscription below it.

Palmer recognised the man depicted easily enough. It was Shakespeare clutching a quill in case anyone mistook him, as Palmer thought they well might for a shopkeeper anxious for custom. It reminded him of old Mansfield the draper.

He translated the Latin.

'The judgement of Nestor, the spirit of Socrates, the art of Virgil ... Olympus has him now.'

Overblown claims, ludicrous in Palmer's opinion.

He turned to Dr Hall with a questioning look.

'The enthusiasm of some of his more literary friends,' Hall explained.

'Ably translated – by you?'

Hall coloured underneath his riding tan.

Palmer read aloud from the closing couplet.

'Sith all, that he hath writ/Leaves living art, but page, to serve his wit.'

'A clever play on words, Dr Hall, page as record, page as servant. Your father-in-law would have approved. We have a page here today....'

'We do?'

Palmer guided him towards young Davenant who was giving an account of his acting and writing experiences to listeners wearing their 'how interesting, I've never heard that before' faces.

'This is Dr Hall,' Palmer said to the young man, cutting him off in full flow. 'Mr Shakespeare's son-in-law, who knew him well. Master Davenant here is a great admirer of the Ovid of Stratford.'

Hall appeared a little startled both by the introduction and by the name he knew from Oxford. Palmer left him and the boy to make the best of it – he had business with Hemmings and Condell.

There was no reason he should want to know anything more about the collected works of the genius above them on the wall, not since he had been paid off but his curiosity was getting the better of him.

Condell was forthcoming.

'Jaggard is print-print-printing away, all nine hundred and odd pages of it. We had hoped it would be ready for the autumn.'

'And it won't be?'

'No. Old William Jaggard is dying, to the distraction of his son Isaac but that's only part of it. Other than printing the King's Bible nothing on this scale has been published for years. We hope for November when the

Court gathers for Christmas. Young Jaggard has recruited Ned Blount to help....'

... a name Palmer recalled from his Revels days, another survivor, a publisher–cum-bookseller with some interest in Shakespeare but more in the long-lost Marlowe, whoever he had been.

'Blount is to sell the book from his shop in St Paul's Churchyard. The talk is of seven hundred copies and more if all goes well.'

Big money Palmer quickly calculated, especially for the publishers if two hundred was breakeven.

'You were pushing at an open door, Mr Palmer.'

'How so?'

'When we were here last year, in Stratford.....'

'Performing?'

'Yes, or rather, no – the Town Council gave us money not to, Puritans you see. Times *have* changed, here and elsewhere. In discussion with Dr Hall we decided we had to do something. For us it was to do with the plays, for him as a proper tribute to the paterfamilias. You see, they are lay rectors of this church, the family, on account of owning a share of church tithes, something William secured to provide for him and his family in his retirement. In addition to regular income it brings certain privileges.'

'Burial and monumentalisation inside the church?'

... a measure of named security inside while awaiting the last trump rather than an unmarked chance in the graveyard outside. A doggerel inscription on the playwright's grave nearby had been Palmer's clue, bearing its interdiction to anyone thinking of digging its occupant up in times to come.

Condell's eyes smiled shrewdly.

'Everything came together and in something of a hurry. But as you can see, coming together it is. Janssen's bust, as you have seen, is up. There is only one task left.'

Palmer's eyes asked what that might be.

'The image for the folio; we have to take back to Master Jaggard's engraver a suitable image.'

'What did the bust-maker work from?'

'Master Janssen? He's in London, next door to the Globe playhouse in Southwark. He worked from sight.'

This acquaintance in life was no explanation to Palmer even if the surname rang a bell – a sculptor of a similar name had done the Benefactor's monument in the Charterhouse Chapel for which he was feeling no home-sickness. It felt good to be out and about in the world.

'Truth to tell, Mr Palmer, the bust we see before us, it has existed for some years. Our friend Shakespeare had it done....'

'In his lifetime?'

'... a year or two before he died. You see he once gave Janssen a commission for a large monument from a Stratford friend.'

Palmer followed the pointing finger to a nearby recumbent figure on a generous tomb.

Condell chuckled.

'Sixty pounds the friend left in his will.'

'A huge amount.'

Palmer hadn't earned sixty pounds in the last ten years, including the Jaggard deal.

'Not for an inveterate moneylender like the late friend.'

Both men raised their eyebrows. The old Christian proscription against usury continued to leave its mark even if it was regularly disobeyed.

'The bust of Shakespeare?'

Palmer's question was self-evident.

'No, that did not cost sixty pounds, more like twenty.'

'Dr Hall?' Palmer suggested, looking in the physician's direction.

'I think,' Henry Condell began to say, 'I think that Will hoped the bust would come to him gratis in recognition of the other commission.'

'But it didn't.'

'No. We rescued it from Janssen's workshop after we last saw you.'

'And Dr Hall paid?'

'Half. Half came from the fee Jaggard paid us.'

'Our friend Hemmings insisted,' Palmer joked.

Condell's eyes twinkled while admitting nothing.

'We still need an image for the Folio of plays, the bust is here, the sculptor is no longer to be found. Do you have any influence with his daughter Mrs Hall?'

'The Duchess, Her Grace had the great condescension to say to me....'

Palmer interrupted whatever in Davenant's mouth the Double Duchess had said when he joined the small group standing around the young page. It consisted of Mrs Hall and her daughter Elizabeth, her name remembered from the encounter on the road with her father.

The girl was silent, intent on admiring the young attractive storyteller. Mrs Hall was not.

'Mr Palmer, we never thought to see you in Stratford again.'

Palmer looked her over. Gone was Susanna the girl of seventeen from the generation before, the one who had trembled in Palmer's room over the future of her father when he was in trouble with the powers-that-be over open rebellion on the streets of London pricked on by his suspect play. The characteristic Shakespeare auburn hair was hidden under a matron's bonnet and flecking with grey. The eyes were as bright, the mouth tighter as if it had learned either discretion or sharp speech or both.

'All was well which turned out so,' he suggested.

Would she leave it there?

'What brings you here?'

This was *not* the opportunity to open the question of Davenant's paternity, Palmer conveyed in a warning glance to his young companion.

'Young William over there, I am his guardian,' he half-truthed. 'No doubt he's told you he is a page in a noble household.'

'... of Her Grace the Duchess of Richmond & Lennox....'

The voice came from Elizabeth. To Palmer it sounded like her mother's twenty years ago.

Mrs Hall flashed a look at her – she should not speak out of turn, not to strangers and certainly not to this one. Elizabeth dropped her eyes.

Palmer pretended not to notice.

'Master William here is ... bookish,' he said.

'Stage-struck more like,' said Mrs Hall.

'Young men will be.'

A young William Shakespeare once had been.

'He was brought up in Oxford.'

'We know all about the Davenants,' Mrs Hall said with a hint of asperity.

'Both his parents are dead as I assume you must know too so I undertook to accompany him home to Oxford, and here when he showed an interest in visiting the birthplace of the immortal Shakespeare.'

'And where will you take him next?'

The meaning was clear.

'I shall return him to the Duke and Duchess.'

Palmer decided it was time to ask a question.

'Our actor friends are interested in an image of your father for an engraving to introduce the Folio of collected works which I had some *small* part in arranging.'

Mrs Hall's left eyebrow rose at the claim as if to say 'and some small part of the earnings, earnings we have seen nothing of.'

'There is one. I cannot part with it,' she said.

'I see.'

Palmer thought quickly.

'Would you be prepared to show it ... if not to me,' he said hastily, 'to my young friend William?'

The girl showed willing to go and fetch it.

'Elizabeth, go to your father!'

The girl obeyed.

Palmer took Susanna Hall aside.

'Mrs Hall, William is already promised. If you were prepared to grant my request....'

Susannah's eyebrow shot up again. Did she know the rumour about her father and Jane Davenant, Palmer wondered?

'I shall speak to my husband,' Mrs Hall said, looking no less severe.

~ 9 ~

AVENANT AND PALMER walked to the appointment in the building which fronted New Place onto the high street. They found Dr Hall there on his own. Mrs Hall had chosen to remain in the manor house behind, where the family lived.

Hall wasted no time on civilities. He took out an object of an unusual size, neither a miniature which it copied in style nor a fuller-sized portrait. It was oval in shape, the size of the average face. It presented a double image.

Palmer looked more closely at it.

The face in the foreground he recognised instantly. It was Henry Wriothesley, Lord Southampton, fair-faced, long-tressed, brilliant-eyed and above all young – '*aetatis suae 20*'.

Behind him was a darker face, male, saturnine, brown-eyed, brown-haired, age given as '29 years'.

The tunic of the young lord was prettily decorated. His shadow behind dressed dark and plain. Relationship was being expressed, but what was it? Pupil and tutor? Innocence and dark spirit?

'Who are they?' Davenant asked.

'Mr Palmer?'

Palmer answered the Doctor. He identified Southampton, adding: 'The man behind is, I presume, William Shakespeare.'

Hall nodded, pursing his lips.

'It was among my father-in-law's possessions, in his private chest opened after his death.'

'I don't think printing an image featuring Southampton would be wise,' Palmer said, remembering the trouble the publication of Shakespeare's private sonnets had caused a dozen years earlier, returning the Earl unwillingly to the public eye as the adored young man of a poet's outpouring.

The Earl had gone up in the world – he was now a powerful man, one of those looking for friendship with the Protestant Dutch in war against Catholic Spain contrary to King James's policy. The return of a disappointed Prince Charles and Villiers from their failed Spanish escapade had tipped them into the pro Dutch war camp in order to cover their embarrassment. It made Southampton more of a force than ever, not one to risk offending.

'An image of Shakespeare could be copied all the same,' said Davenant, sizing it up from different angles. 'I could do it.'

Hall withdrew it protectively.

Palmer drew the young man back.

'Copy the bust in the church instead,' he said quietly.

The image at the front of the unbound Folio which Palmer was leafing through weeks later in Blount's bookstall in St Paul's Churchyard was not the best. Nor was it drawn from life whatever Ben Jonson claimed in his exhortation to book-buyers on the opening page.

The young engraver had stylised Davenant's sketch even further. The impression was of a younger man than the bust. Eyes and shoulders were unbalanced in a faint attempt at perspective by an artist addressing his subject slightly from the right but used to working flat. It was a wonky, two-dimensional cartoon staring out at Palmer. The author deserved better.

The weather was Christmas-cold. Copies were selling for between fifteen to twenty shillings each depending on the binding sought. He was not tempted to raid his purse which had already been depleted by an extra offering in the Chapel of the Charterhouse. The Preacher no longer disputed his excuses for absence, he resorted to a more rewarding practice.

'Go away as often as you like,' he said as he pocketed Palmer's shillings in fine.

'The Lord taketh away....'

Palmer was muttering this to himself as he made his way south through Smithfield Market, scene of fairs and butchery, of beasts and sometimes of men when the State saw fit and the people wanted entertainment. He was on his way to St Paul's. Walking through the Cathedral and all its unholy goings on, coming out on the south side he found Carter Lane, home of his favourite drinking hole, the Bell Inn.

The old tapster, sole relict of Palmer's ancient landlord gave him a warning.

'There's an ol' feller askin' after yer.'

'So sorry, Mr Palmer,' the Chief Minister's one-time official apologised from his stool by the fire. 'I went for my pension on quarter day, Christmas day. There was a difficulty.'

Palmer stood over the old man. His hair was sparse, his beard was white and ragged. His smile was as apologetic as his brown eyes were docile. He reminded Palmer of a neglected old household pet.

Palmer ordered food and drink for two including a cup of sack, his guest's favourite drink in the old days. The old man pecked and sipped. He was entitled to better, Palmer reckoned, better than he himself deserved at the Charterhouse but there was one problem, the old boy's religion. He would starve rather than acclaim with his lips the new rite which had displaced the old faith in his heart.

'So the Crown is running out of money again,' Palmer said.

The old official pushed the allegation aside.

'An oversight I'm sure. If His Majesty knew....'

'God knows, old friend, but how many big brains have been applied to this problem of the royal finances? The Chief Minister was working on it in your day.'

'Greville too,' the old man murmured into the wine he realised he used to like, 'when he was Chancellor of the Exchequer. Good man, Fulke Greville. Broke his health over it, just like my old master. Do you know him?'

As if he would, Palmer laughed quietly to himself. The old man rehearsed the story.

'A Warwickshire man, made his name in the Marches, the Welsh borders, bosom friend of Sir Philip Sidney, soldier and poet. My master Cecil took against him though I could never see why....'

Was this the first word of disloyalty to a sacred memory Palmer had ever heard the old public servant utter? Poverty aided truth.

'... unless it was his writing a suggestive drama against tyranny.'

Another tricky playwright Palmer remarked privately. The Stuarts stood closer to the tyranny than they ever did to the democracy of the Greeks. *Mon*-archy after all, the rule by one.

'Greville would have been Lord Treasurer if his health had stood up. All the same, he *is* Baron Brooke.'

Of Brooke House in Holborn, Palmer realised, over the road from young Davenant in Ely House. He tried to place this Lord in the shifting sands of politics. Was there a sniff of the old, lethal Essex connection?

'A friend of Lord Southampton's?' Palmer asked, using his surest test of how sound a man was or wasn't.

'I don't know about that. You know there is talk of Southampton commanding troops to be sent against the Spaniards in the Low Countries?'

The penniless wraith in clothes which were half rags evidently kept up with public policy. Palmer sighed at the news. He had served his soldier's time in the same place, same argument, thirty years ago – a graveyard for English bones, and for what?

He lowered his voice to a whisper.

'Is it true that Southampton still clings to your old faith?'

Water appeared in the old man's rheumy eyes. Sadly not, the shake of his head was meant to say.

'His father and mother did, ardently too.'

'But not him.'

'Oh I think he used to, until he went out on his own. The Cecils took him on as ward. He was drawn into the circle of another of their wards, the late lamented Lord Essex.'

Who has been the champion of the radical wing of the new religion, Palmer did not need to be reminded.

'Now he fights for the Protestant cause, here and on the continent....'

... where the King's daughter and son-in-law were leading the Protestant quarrel with the Habsburg juggernaut, flagbearers of Catholic power. It was an upward, unequal struggle.

'The King never wanted it.'

No, he wouldn't, Palmer understood. War and James were words never connected in the same sentence. His son Charles, now, he was taking a different line after his Spanish fiasco.

'One would not recognise Southampton today....'

Palmer didn't suppose one would. What was he now? Fifty, into life's yellow sere. Not like the image in the portrait he had recently seen in Stratford, green with youth.

'... what with his short hair and beard of military cut.'

Style of the military faction the old official and his master Cecil had worked so hard to control.

'Where do you sleep?' Palmer asked him abruptly.

The look he received gave him no answer and without words there was no bed, no lodging, no roof over his head. This old man on the streets? Palmer was enraged. But not so enraged that he would take the man in. Being half a Good Samaritan would do, any more and he would be in for sainthood. He pulled out a weighty crown, five shillings worth of sustenance. It still left him five pounds to the good.

'Until I get my pension,' the old man insisted, 'only until then.'

Palmer mentioned the Greville name to Emilia. She looked up sharply.

'So you know him?' Palmer asked her.

'Of him,' she said, her eyes returning to her sewing. 'It was in my days with Lady Cumberland.'

Palmer remembered both the time and the woman. She was older than Emilia and devout, separated from her husband, part of a circle of virtuous, literary women which Emilia liked to think she spiritually belonged to once she had given up her racy youth. The Lady was long dead too, dust, dust.

'My Lady was friendly with the Countess of Pembroke, Mary Sidney as was.'

'Philip Sidney's sister. So the Countess and Greville had Sidney in common.'

Emilia laughed at the thought.

'They wrangled over who was the keeper of his memory. There is no Lady Greville,' she added with a significant look. 'I have no way to him, if that's what you're after for young Davenant.'

Palmer didn't see the old official again until the early days of Lent which he spent observing in the Bell Inn. A frail figure, this time washed and combed and in a suit of clothes which bespoke service went almost unrecognised when it came in one afternoon.

The man's first act was to hand over a golden angel worth ten shillings and two half-crowns worth five, as much as Palmer had given him in charity.

'I insist,' the old man said, closing Palmer's hand around the coins.

Palmer ordered drinks on the strength of it before asking about the man's change of fortune.

'It was talking about Fulke Greville when I was with you here at Christmas. He is a man of books. By God's grace I heard he was looking for a librarian and archivist. There is no salary of course....'

'Of course not,' Palmer told himself who knew the way of those with money not wishing to be parted from it. So, the old chap opposite had made his own connection with Greville.

'... but I have clothing, board and lodging; and his books!'

It was a heaven in which the old official now found himself.

'And I have my pension, paid in full. Greville, Lord Brooke was most helpful about that, a word in the right ear if you understand me. There were significant arrears.'

Palmer did understand, glad the old man had at last benefited. And so had he, to the tune of fifteen shillings repaid.

'I have never known your name,' Palmer said, 'your given name.'

He was lying, as if he already knew the surname. It was an old trick of his.

'Ralph,' the old man said, sipping at the goblet of sack bought for him.

The news in Emilia's house was not so good.

Palmer found Miracle and Emilia together waiting for him the following day once his penances in the Charterhouse Chapel were over.

'Tell him, Miracle,' said Emilia.

'The Duke is sick.'

There was only one Duke ever talked of in this house, Richmond & Lennox.

'How sick?'

'He's dead,' Emilia cut in.

'William fears for his place in the household. The talk is that the Duchess will be hard put to maintain a household in the fashion she is accustomed to,' Miracle told him.

'Unless she marries again – for the fourth time.'

Emilia spoke sarcastically.

'I will only marry another of my rank....'

So the Duchess had said to Davenant when he attended her late at night in expectation of another tryst.

'... or the old King himself. It's a disgusting thought but think of the rank, think of the position though God knows I doubt if any position of mine could excite His Majesty....'

The Duchess had laughed gaily.

'... I shall of course leave him to his boyfriends.'

Davenant had thought what it could do for him. He reached out towards her decolletage.

'Not for the time being, my best boy. I must be, how to put it, integer, as a virtuous widow should be.'

Emilia's sarcasm continued unbridled.

'That's not all. Tell him, Miracle.'

The girl cast her eyes down. Her voice quavered. Nothing more came out.

Emilia stepped in.

'Miracle is with child, she is expecting a baby.'

Emilia's eyes glittered with anger as much from memories of her own past as the present news.

Thirty years ago she had been a woman kept in the highest style by one of the most powerful men in the land with jewels, rich living and forty pounds a year, more than Palmer had ever earned. And as he knew she had been playing around with two other men at the same time, that beautiful youth of noble family and the scurrilous playwright seen so recently in the portrait shown to him by Dr Hall. Unwanted pregnancy had done for her, seen her married off in short order to a bully of a husband with no great liking for women; and him no better than a Court musician like her own father despite his aspirations for a military career.

All that history could be seen in her eyes and heard in her voice, all directed towards Palmer.

'*Your* young Master Davenant is going to have to do his duty!'

... which was not going to be easy.

'After His Grace's funeral I am to leave the Duchess's service.'

This was what Davenant had to tell Palmer when the old investigator went to see him in Ely House. The Duchess had made her cold choice.

'Have you any other prospects?'

'I have been working on my verse – there's the beginnings of a play.'

Davenant knew this sounded lame.

Palmer said nothing about the pregnancy. He left the page to the household obsequies for the Duke, crossing a busy road in search of Brooke House.

The old official was surprised in the library, cataloguing books, shelving the newly rebound and building up a pile in need of fresh bindings.

'Mr Palmer!'

Palmer lost no time in explaining his mission.

'He's a bookish boy,' Palmer urged, 'if plays count as books.'

'To some extent, to some extent,' the old man muttered and fluttered his hands. 'Lord Brooke is a man of books, a patron of them, a writer even....'

There was a 'but' coming. Palmer headed it off.

'I understand that His Lordship has never married.'

What was he doing, pimping the boy out?

'His taste is for solitude....'

'It means that he retains a single gentleman's household, far less expensive than a married man's.'

'... because he lives frugally. I, as you know, receive no stipend.'

'Then young Master Davenant will have to become a *successful* writer..........'

It was not something Palmer had ever expected to hear himself say.

'... you used to like the plays as I recall.'

Memory conveniently returned of an encounter with a playwright in a tiring house behind a stage when the old official had been too all-a-twitter to ask for what he really wanted.

Palmer made himself clear.

'My young man needs a proper position while he makes his way.'

The old man began wringing his hands.

'I'll see what can be done,' was all he would say.

'If and when you get the position in Brooke House, you're going to marry Miracle.'

Palmer was not interested in all the excuses in the world Davenant came up with – shouldn't they wait for confirmation of a new post, wouldn't it be better to allow time for him to establish himself with any new master, wasn't it forbidden to marry in Lent or to call the banns?

To each Palmer had an answer including to the last.

'We shall obtain a special marriage licence.'

An interview was arranged at Brooke House. Palmer
made sure he was present even if it meant listening at the
door along with the old official while Fulke Greville put
the young man through his paces.

The Baron's voice was smooth and practised. It
sounded younger than a man in his seventieth year
approaching his biblical three score and ten.

'As I understand it your family were respectable
vintners in Oxford, you have spent time at the University
there and most recently served as a page in the Lennox
household.'

'Richmond & Lennox, sir.'

'Quite so, quite so, a correct title is important even if
it is now, I suppose *vacant*. In the ordinary course, I would
not be looking to add to my household but I understand
that you are an aspirant writer.'

'My interest is in verse applied to the stage, for
example in the play or the masque.'

'The masque? Very *courtly*, I'm sure, and altogether
more safely *allegorical* than the theatre, fewer chances of
any misunderstandings with the Censor.'

Unless you're Ben Jonson Palmer thought to himself
outside the door.

'... plenty of muses, gods and goddesses to remove
the subject matter from the *venalities* of the present age.
What are you working on now?'

'A play for the public or the private stage I hope.'

Davenant described it, at first with retiscence and
then with a growing confidence. He understood it was
essential to persuade the world you were a writer by
saying so, it was half the game.

'Interesting,' Greville said. 'I should like to see some
examples of it.'

'I have some with me.'

You cheeky imp, Palmer thought who hadn't suggested it.

Silence followed, enough time for a reader to study a page properly.

'Your metre is sound,' Greville's voice was heard to say, 'there's good use of language and imagery, perhaps a little florid, obscure even here and there but a young man might be forgiven for that. Whether it translates into dramatic action I cannot judge from what little there is before me.'

A painful pause was broken by the same voice.

'... but yes, there is matter here. Perhaps I might help you with it. I have written for the public in my day. Would you be averse to suggestions? Some writers are, they believe they know best.'

'I am happy to take all the advice I can from those with experience.'

Right answer, Palmer agreed outside the door.

'How old are you?'

'Just turned eighteen, sir.'

'Man's estate, not in Law but in practice. You are a little old to be called a page but I am sure we can find you some responsibilities suitable for a young gentleman of my household and a modest stipend to go with it. If you assist my Librarian I am sure he will be tolerant over time needed for your writing which I shall expect to see and – what is the modern word? – ah, yes, *criticise*, helpfully of course.'

'It would be most welcome, sir.'

Palmer thumped his fist into the other palm in celebration; then he and the old official retreated quietly before the door could open.

'Your reason for the special licence?'

The Bishop's Clerk in the consistory court did not look up from his papers at the blushing Davenant in front of him. Palmer intervened.

'The pair are betrothed. The bride is since with child.'

The two older men looked at each other with frank understanding. Betrothal, handfasting, whatever it was called brought with it certain customs, certain natural rights which might run ahead of solemnisation at the altar steps.

'Name of bride,' the clerk asked, pen poised.

'Miracle,' Palmer said. 'Her mother had no surname to my knowledge – I am the girl's godfather. She was brought up as foster-daughter in the household of John and Jane Davenant, the groom's parents, both deceased. A respectable Oxford family in a good way of trade.'

The Clerk looked up and put his pen down.

'Miracle? Did I hear you right?'

'It was how she was baptised. I was present.'

'Miracle?'

The Clerk tutted again.

'There is a problem?' Palmer asked.

'A problem there most certainly is. My right reverend master the Lord Bishop could not countenance it.'

'Why not?' asked Palmer, bringing his purse into view.

'The child was born in Oxford you say? In Oxford, no doubt matters are ... other. But such a name here, it is blasphemous.'

'It *was* a miracle, I was there.'

Palmer could not help his testiness, remembering a stillborn child or so it had seemed brought to life by the cold waters of a river.

'That is for God to decide or for our reverend priests. Yes, here it will be considered blasphemous or at best an example of the nomenclature of dissenters, those who follow the true faith but refuse to do so in the prescribed manner.'

A manner he represented.

Palmer fingered his purse.

'How do we resolve this?'

The Clerk saw the purse.

'We enter a more appropriate name.'

'Such as?'

'Why not Mary?'

Palmer stopped himself from snorting at the irony.

'Mother of God. I see.'

The Clerk looked scandalised.

'Mother of Jesus Christ, his only Son, our Lord!'

Davenant began to protest.

Palmer kicked him.

'Mary it is. And the fee?'

'Most usually....'

The Clerk named the amount, hinting that was he was doing was 'most unusual'.

Palmer pushed the fee across with two shilling pieces added.

The nib of the pen began to scratch busily on the parchment.

~ 10 ~

'DO YOU TAKE this man....'
Miracle gave out a confident 'I do.' She was dressed in her Sunday best which disguised her condition.

The company in church was small, restricted to bride and groom, Palmer as best man and one of the witnesses, Emilia Lanier as matron. The other witness, Henry Lanier made pleasing sounds on the small church organ for a bridal introit and exit. Davenant's brothers and sisters had not been invited.

The last and most sentimental guest was the old official who dabbed at his eyes throughout.

'What we shall say to my Lord Brooke I do not know.'

Palmer did, who had already taken the precaution to go and see him.

Greville was not best pleased at the news.

His long-nosed, unbearded, gallic-looking face was set into the stern image of the man of the toga rather than breastplate and sword. A tale of youthful gallantry was not going to get its way with him.

'You say you are the boy's guardian.'

'In a manner of speaking.'

Greville gave Palmer a look to say that 'a manner of speaking' was not good enough.

'I shall throw him out on his ear. He, you must have known this *doxy* was with child.'

Palmer said nothing.

'I will not have squalling brats in my house!'

Palmer's voice was measured in response.

'The child will be fostered nearby.'

Palmer would deal with Emilia about that separately. He didn't look forward to it.

'I will not have the mother here either, she must live elsewhere.'

The discussion over that with Emilia would be even more fractious. But Palmer took heart. There was something in the boy Greville wanted to keep hold of.

'The boy's writing....' Palmer began to say, feeling his way forward.

'He's good,' Greville admitted, 'or he will be when I've finished with him. It's a terrible shame he has cast himself into the arms of Woman. They suck away a man's powers.'

The boy had promised him a personal poem when he felt he was ready, 'when I can prove my numbers smooth and mighty as my love,' he had sweetly put it.

He was too valuable to be wasted on baby-making.

'Marriage is an honourable estate,' said Palmer who had not tried it himself and knew the man opposite hadn't either.

Greville growled yet when he sent Palmer on his way it was with one precious concession – agreement that the boy's place was safe for the time being.

Emilia did not erupt as Palmer had feared she might. He wondered why.

'My boy Henry....' she started to say.

Henry Lanier was a married man himself. He had finally wedded his Joyce in the August of the previous year in the bride's church of St Andrew's by-the-Wardrobe, near Blackfriars just inside the City walls.

There had been more Mansfields present than the Bassanos and Laniers – those who were not working and therefore free – who provided the music. Among the groom's relations Palmer spotted the moneylender from Deptford. Neither man acknowledged the other, the day was not one for business.

The dowry of one hundred and fifty pounds was paid promptly, a highly satisfactory result on both sides.

'... Henry has been offered lodgings,' Emilia said, 'nearer the Court in Greenwich.'

There was no child for Henry on the way, that much Palmer knew and his new location out east was a matter of convenience. Whitehall was central and easily accessible by river as was Hampton Court out west. The Thames was the regular thoroughfare for Court servants. Plenty of Bassanos and Laniers lived in Greenwich. The river was their second home as they moved around the Capital in royal service.

'... so there is room here for Miracle and her child but only if....'

'If what?'

'... only if her husband is to be of the visiting kind.'

Not under Emilia's feet, Palmer understood.

'... but mark my words, child does not mean children.'

They would cross that bridge when they came to it, Palmer told himself.

'... and there must be an arrangement over costs of lodging and living.'

There had been one unusual figure at Henry Lanier's wedding feast. When he saw him, Palmer did a double-take – the man was the spitting image of Alphonso Lanier, Emilia's late and unlamented husband. He couldn't be of course. The man's dress was richer than Alphonso's had ever been, the latest in Court style with beard combed thin and pointed. It jutted out from the chin of a face fleshy from good living in high places rather than the liquor of the alehouse which Alphonso had liked, so Palmer judged.

'Nicholas Lanier,' the man had introduced himself, 'cousin of the bridegroom.'

Of course, son of one of Alphonso's brothers, all of them Court musicians only this one a few years older than Henry and one who had done especially well. This was Henry's mentor and his hope of promotion to Court musician.

Nicholas Lanier had owed his own start to Robert Cecil, Chief Minister – a recommendation to Palmer who had worked for the man himself. He began as a lutenist and a singer and songwriter, Henry had once told him, contributing to Court entertainments. Within no time at all he was staging masques, writing all the music, designing the sets and costumes.

The one-man-band alternative to Inigo Jones, Palmer reckoned remembering Ben Jonson's stage-designing partner, a cheaper, less quarrelsome option for masque-fanciers, reliable too. And he acted pleasant unlike his cousin, the late Alphonso.

'The go-between,' Palmer explained himself, jerking a nod towards Draper Mansfield.

Nicholas Lanier smiled, an honest one.

'Yes, I heard that Henry had done well over the dowry. Well done, Mr Palmer.'

'Will Henry's position be confirmed at Court?'

Lanier replied with attractive confidence.

'Henry is close to me, I am close to the Prince of Wales whose Master of the King's Musick I shall be ... when the terrible hour comes.'

Lanier smiled, this time more politically.

'I had heard you were interested in more than music,' Palmer said.

Lanier nodded gracefully.

'His Royal Highness has entrusted me with a mission.'

Palmer waited to be told.

'Our Prince wishes to enlarge the royal collection of paintings. I have hopes of a great acquisition from the Gonzagas of Mantua. I have my eye on their Mantegnas – do you know him? No? A wonderful artist – the colours, the composition, the scale and the imagination of his classical and biblical subjects. But music is my first love, I confess. It is my *trade*.'

Lanier's cheeks dimpled with humour under their courtly pink gloss.

Henry would do well to remain close to him was Palmer's assessment.

'*A Game at Chess*? Whyever would I want to see that?'

Palmer's protest was sincere when William Davenant tried to recruit him for a play-visit to the Globe on Bankside in the dog days of August.

'It's a huge success, one of Middleton's best. All the characters are cast as chess pieces – White King, Black Bishop, Black Knight and so on. It's an allegory.'

Palmer remembered Thomas Middleton and his thin top lip, co-author with Shakespeare of the *Timon* play back in the day when the Chief Minister had wanted to speak in parables to the King about his regal overspending.

'What's the allegory about?'

'Spain of course, even if the King's Men flatly deny it.'

They would, Palmer told himself.

'All the black pieces are Spanish, the white English. The Black Knight, for example is the former Spanish Ambassador, Gondemar....'

'Which the King's Men no doubt deny.'

'Yes, they do but he's unmistakeable – the players have even bought some of his cast-off wardrobe to wear onstage. The Black King is Philip of Spain.'

'Hold on, hold on, this is,' Palmer struggled for the word, 'prohibited. Living Christian monarchs must not be shown onstage, it's the Censor's rule ... at least it was in my time in that office.'

'It still is but here's the rub. The play was passed by the censor, by Herbert, the new Master of the Revels.'

Palmer smelled double-dealing. No doubt the black pieces representing Spain would be up to no good. He asked Davenant what sort.

'Yes, seduction and perversion....'

Why on earth was the Master of the Revels allowing it?

'This Herbert, bound to be related to the Wilton Herberts? And so to Lord Pembroke?'

'I reckon so.'

Lord Chamberlain Pembroke, anti-Spanish, looking for war and so with the compliance of his Censor-relative using the players' mouths for some political provocation?

'The Spanish Embassy has complained to King James himself,' Davenant said. 'Everybody's going to see it before it's banned. The King's Men are putting it on every day while they can.'

Palmer refused to join in.

Autumn brought the baptism of a lusty boy for the Davenants, named William after his father to which Palmer added private speculation, that it honoured the unspoken grandfather too.

The anti-Spanish party had its way.

War was declared on Spain. It brought immediate fighting in the Low Countries. A familiar name marched away to it – Henry Wriothesley, Earl of Southampton, leading one of the English regiments when he had expected to command the entire force. His eldest son rode alongside him.

Palmer watched them go by to the beat of the drum and the squeal of the fife enjoying their hour of admiration in the public eye. The grim reality of trenches and ramparts and the squalor of death and disfigurement as the true companions to glory would follow soon enough.

Old memories stirred disgust in him.

Southampton's boy riding alongside his father distracted Palmer. He was the image of the fair youth his father had once been, as the poet had promised all those years ago.

Palmer's eye caught the noble Earl's. There was no recognition. Looking at the man, looking at the boy, why was it men never learned?

November brought back news of plague among the troops abroad. It also brought rare tears to Emilia Lanier's eyes when Palmer made a visit to Miracle and her baby.

'Southampton is dead! Plague, they say. He was bringing back his son, dead too. Imagine what the Countess is feeling!'

Palmer could not. Age had gnarled the Countess's husband. He was not the image of his youth, he was a different Southampton, a politician ardent in the Protestant cause, an ambitious courtier, a soldier first and foremost, everything such a scion of nobility should be engrafted onto the trunk of State, far removed from the poet's adored one so many years ago.

Now he and his son were to be translated into pompous inscriptions on tombs out at the family estate in Hampshire. The second son was unexpectedly to be the new Earl. Second sons – like Prince Charles, old King

Henry Six Wives himself, they were an unpredictable commodity.

Still Emilia wept, for Southampton, for herself, for times past and lost. How many others did, Palmer wondered, victims to the cool Southampton charm?

December brought more news of State of family interest to the mistress of the Lanier household.

'Prince Charles is to marry. The bride is Princess Henrietta Maria of France. This will be good news for my son,' Emilia said, mindful of his Court ambitions.

Marriage celebrations would mean more work for musicians close to the royal Prince. A larger establishment beckoned, more positions for his would-be servants.

Spring served a fatal stroke.

Palmer heard it earlier than the little household in Clerkenwell by a royal proclamation from the Guildhall, home of the City Government.

'The King is dead. Long live the King!'

James Stuart dead, another worn-out quinquegenerian like Palmer.

He and the King were of an age, the old investigator reflected as he walked back to his lodgings in the Charterhouse. It was as if rungs of the ladder above and below him were being sawn away one by one. He had lived to see a third monarch. His father, the holy fool had seen four with all their wild oscillations of faith. The new king had a Catholic wife – what might that mean?

The Stuarts had their feet well under the table was Palmer's opinion. All Charles had to do was wear the crown, humour Parliament, keep his bride's Catholicism unostentatious and father sons.

It ought not, he reasoned, to be too difficult to achieve.

The new King was not crowned until the year after his accession. Just as it had for his father, a new bout of plague ruled out large public gatherings which were prohibited by Government order.

King Charles the First, never a royal name in England or Scotland was crowned in a miserable February. For once Palmer expected his position as a gentleman-pensioner to do him some good in getting a view of the pageant before the ceremony. The Preacher had thought so too, but no, word came that the new King was not much for parading himself before the people, like his father in that respect, yet unlike him since James had at least put himself out to try. Worse, the equally tiny French Queen did not at all agree to being crowned alongside her spouse under the new and to her, false religion.

'Her religious advisers told her so,' Henry Lanier, finally appointed to the Court told Palmer.

And the new King's response to his wife?

'His Majesty sent her bishop and scores of clerical hangers on back to where they came from in France. He had to have them physically ejected! It is a marriage which....'

'... is in need of encouragement?'

Lanier laughed at Palmer's suggestion. Like his father, Charles was closest to George Villiers, Duke of Buckingham whose bedroom continued nearest to the new King's as it had been to the old.

Palmer brought back to mind an image of the two gallants dancing together in the masque. Like a previous dancing favourite under the old Queen, rash Essex, Villiers could not be faulted for the shape of his legs. His touch in politics was less sure, just like Essex too.

Henry Lanier had enjoyed a closer view of the Coronation than many.

'The old Archbishop was so feeble that when he announced His Majesty, all chrismed and crowned, nobody heard him so there was no shout of acclamation!'

Ominous.

'And the Queen?'

The eager voice was young Davenant's.

Lanier replied.

'She looked on from above, she took no part.'

Palmer gave Davenant a sharp look. He changed the subject.

'Will this play of yours ever be finished?' he asked him. 'Have you given it a title?'

'I call it *The Cruel Brother*. It is a tragedy......'

Davenant's melodramatic sweep of his arm imitated an imaginary cloak.

'... and yes, it is to be performed, that is it will be when I've finished it. Lord Brooke has told me so. We are to have a *private* reading in Brooke House.'

Emilia Lanier, uncharacteristically silent in the corner of the room, spoke up.

'My Ladies used to hold private readings for prayerful texts....'

Palmer laughed out loud. Emilia shot him an angry look.

'.... and for plays, if their matter was suitable.'

'Did women play women's parts?'

Davenant was keen to know.

'I suppose they must have – Lady Richmond & Lennox certainly did. I should like it to be so for my play. I wish to be the first writer to introduce women onto the public stage!'

'Fat chance of that,' snorted Palmer. 'In England, women may dance provided it's not on the public stage but act, they may not. Even if they could, think who your patron is, the good, wifeless Baron Brooke. If you want women playing plays in his house, I wish you the best of luck!'

~ 11 ~

'IT'S AS BIG as the whole of our Tavern was in Oxford,' Miracle whispered in awe as she stood in the main hall of Brooke House.

Emilia Lanier was equally impressed.

'As big as the houses I was used to in my time with the Lord Chamberlain in the days of the old Queen.'

'The Crown Tavern had twenty rooms!'

'Remember, we are only here on sufferance. We sit at the back of the hall,' Emilia reminded her lodger.

The flame of candles in freestanding candelabras threw soft light across the hall onto its dark, deep-polished panelling and its rippling tapestries.

In the middle of the hall a group of men gathered in discussion. William Davenant had brought together all the useful friends he could muster. Henry Lanier was responsible for a small consort of music. Ralph the Librarian was in charge of the play rolls issued to each actor. Two elderly men were also involved. One the women recognised – Palmer; the other they did not.

'Good of you to come, Master Hemmings,' Palmer was heard saying to the veteran actor.

'I came at Lord Brooke's invitation.'

The truth was he had come just in case the play was any good and the writer a find. Good writers were as rare as hen's teeth, always had been.

'So what's it about?' he asked.

Palmer thought for a moment.

'A tale of rank and position, love, jealousy and revenge. Foreste, the cruel brother of the title has been raised from low estate by Count Lucio who is the minion of the Duke.'

Both men exchanged looks. There had been minions aplenty under the Stuarts culminating in Villiers, a minion-exalted who was now playing mentor to the young Monarch.

'Lucio secretly marries Foreste's sister, Corsa, simple, beautiful, chaste but low-born like her brother.'

'Of course,' Hemmings rumbled, 'I've brought one of our boys from the King's Men to read her part. Our boys *can* read you know.'

'The Duke forgives Lucio and invites Corsa to the Court. He secretly lusts after her - so he sends Lucio away on diplomatic business.'

'All very David and Bathsheba,' said Hemmings, happy to have a biblical precedent whenever rulers were presented onstage behaving badly – one could never tell which way the Censor might jump these days especially after the recent trouble with the Middleton play.

'The Duke ravishes Corsa. Her husband Lucio discovers it, tells her brother Foreste who ... slits Corsa's wrists for the sake of family honour.'

'As we can trust your Italians to do! What happens in the way of revenge? There has to be revenge.'

Nothing originally from what Palmer had read, flattered by young Davenant into doing so. He'd told the boy it couldn't just end there, there had to be retribution, it was the law of tragedy from the age of the Greeks which Palmer knew best. Apparently Lord Brooke had said the same thing.

'The Duke is penitent and begs for death yet Lucio forgives him, so does Foreste.'

'Very *christian* of them.'

'There's a brawl – organised by an evil creature of the Court turned assassin, I forget why. The Duke, Lucio and Foreste are mortally wounded. They die clasping hands.'

'Cue bodies lifted up on high and carried off to solemn music,' said Hemmings. 'Works every time. I particularly remember it in that last scene from *Hamlet*, when was it? Twenty-five years ago....'

A sharp look from Palmer discouraged the threatened anecdote.

'Well, it sounds a good plot,' Hemmings conceded. 'Let's see if the boy Davenant can put it over.'

Fulke Greville, Baron Brooke made his entrance into the hall last of all.

He sat down in the position of honour and authority in a large chair positioned in the centre of the room opposite a low dais set up to function as the stage. Hall doors behind served for entrances and exits.

Greville was dressed in his best long robe, fur-trimmed to give ample protection from draughts. Around him sat on stools were other gentlemen of his household, Hemmings among them with another guest.

'Mr Endymion Porter,' Ralph the Librarian confided to Palmer. 'A servant of His Grace the Duke of Buckingham, Master of his Horse; despite that a man of letters and a great patron of poets.'

He appeared an amenable sort of man judging by the smile on his face when talking to Greville. He remained as friendly when he was introduced to Davenant. To Palmer he looked more the sturdy country squire, rubicund face and all than a denizen of City or Court.

'So welcome Master Maecenas,' he heard Greville said to his visitor.

Porter smiled good-naturedly enough at the tribute to his cultural standing.

Davenant was not to be left out in paying high-flown compliments.

'I can only hope one day to aspire to Virgil's heaven-directed verse.'

'Then let us see what you have for us, young man....'

The great men taking the best stools, Palmer, Ralph, Emilia and Miracle contented themselves with low benches at the back of the hall.

Greville's beringed right hand glinted as it gave the signal for the action to begin. Backstage right one of the doors opened. Two figures entered, Count Lucio and his gentleman Foreste.

Palmer immediately recognised Davenant self-cast as the Count. Equipped with a playroll in his hand he spoke largely without reference to it. How many times had he written, read and re-read the words in front of him? His Foreste, played by another gentleman of the household was more studied and dependant on the script. Davenant spoke naturally, his colleague how he thought an actor ought to, loudly and not always promptly on cue.

The opening scene did what it should, establish who was who and in what relation as well as what the matter of the play was to be – Lucio's wish to marry Foreste's sister Corsa despite her low standing.

A villain, Castruchio was quickly introduced and a quarrel. Castruchio and Foreste set to – impressive swordplay which the two combatants had obviously rehearsed more than the words. A good fight was an excellent ornament to a play, that much Palmer knew.

The plot rolled out in sonorous verse studded with jewel-lines , self-consciously proverbial.

'*The way to honour is not evermore / the way to hell; a virtuous man may climb.*'

Soft-gloved hands in the audience pattered applause at the sentiment. Palmer's ungloved hands did not.

'*... some employ their times in wanton exercise / Masques and Revels....*'

The applause turned warmer and more knowing.

Music played – Henry Lanier and friends from the side of the stage – to introduce the fair young Corsa.

... but no Corsa came on.

The consort of music laid down a second chord to introduce her. No-one came. The chord repeated.

A voice, crystal clear and sweet poured out, not from the stage front or back but from the benches at the back of the hall. It was a young woman's voice not a boy's, as pure but gentler.

'*My heart with gladness sees my love.*'

The consort followed the voice. All hell broke loose.

'I only sang it because Henry wrote it,' Miracle explained afterwards to Palmer and Emilia, speaking over the hubbub created by her intrusion into the play.

'What is the matter, what *is* the matter?'

The irritated voice was Greville's, asking for an explanation.

Davenant disappeared backstage. He came back with it.

'There's something wrong with our boy player – violent coughing, feverish forehead.'

People looked at each other in consternation. The latest bout of plague had not long died down.

'Hemmings, get that boy home,' Greville ordered. '*Now* what are we going to do?'

'I could *read* the part.'

A voice, male, elderly and timorous spoke up.

Greville waved Ralph the Librarian aside.

'There is someone who knows it,' Davenant said from the stage, 'someone who has read it over many times with me.'

'And that would be?'

'My wife Miracle.'

The disparaging snort everyone heard was from old Hemmings as he strode out of the hall.

'*According to the age of monarchies / they – the French – are fully ripe.*'

The tilt at the French being ripe for revolution went down well in the small Blackfriars Theatre inside the walls of the City of London.

The audience was select, well-to-do as they had to be given the prices charged for winter entertainment indoors, six times what the King's Men charged at the summertime Globe.

The target France was England's oldest and newest enemy in the policy of the new King Charles and his Chief Minister Villiers, despite England's young French Queen.

The theory of the inevitable corruptibility of monarchy as a human rather a divine system of rule was the published view of Baron Brooke, not that it ever did any good against the prevailing Stuart philosophy of God-given absolute rule. The King could do no wrong was the rule.

Palmer reckoned young D'Avenant, as he now styled himself in front of these courtly spectators had done well to shove Brooke's risky claim into the French domain. A line inserted about the over-maturity of the English monarchy not to be expected for another three hundred years was likely to have appeased the Censor – who could care what happened in 1928? The more sophisticated the audience, the more a writer was allowed to suggest. It was in the public theatre in front of the numerous masses that the Government was at its most apprehensive. Shades of *Richard II*, a generation before, mounted at the Globe to get the mob in the mood for regicide still hovered over dramatic consciences.

Onstage Corsa was making her marriage with Count Lucio.

'*I know this match was made in heaven; and not / provoked by any sinful art in me.*'

The boy player was back on duty. Old John Hemmings had seen enough in Brooke House, sufficient to get the play licensed for performance by his King's Men.

'As for that stuff and nonsense about Davenant's wife appearing on the stage,' John Hemmings told Palmer, 'the Master of the Revels wouldn't stand for it, our licence to perform would be withdrawn and our royal patent with it....'

The new Master, Herbert was reckoned much more directive than either of his predecessors.

'... and as for the audience, forget what the men might like, the women wouldn't have it! No, my wife left the acting to me, to both her husbands! The very thought!'

Onstage, the Duke appeared to accept the marriage and then not, for reasons of his own wounded love. This drew Palmer's attention, the suspicion that the Duke was jealous of the girl not the man. The comparison to slobbering old King James was made perfectly clear. It reminded the old investigator of William Shakespeare and his tales of bonds between older and younger men, all very Greek. Was it was because Davenant was living in an ambivalent world in the Brooke household? Palmer imagined he knew how to look after himself. What if it was what he wanted, what he enjoyed?

It didn't bother Palmer. It would Miracle.

Onstage Count Lucio was sent to the front.

The Duke soliloquised in self-reproach and self-justification.

'He that repents e'er he commits a fault / doth like a thirsty sinner store his soul/ with mercy.'

The royal mood grew grimmer.

'What I did mean / adultery at first, will now I fear/ become a rape.'

After the deed, to Palmer's approval committed decorously offstage, the Duke offered up remorse.

'O traitor lust / that leads us with encouragement to fight / and when we have discharged our veins for thee / we are besieged with thoughts that more perplex us / than the former.'

It was a clumsy way of putting it.

'The expense of spirit in a waste of shame is lust in action....'

... forced its way into Palmer's memory, from sonnets he had once confiscated and then had published written by a better wordsmith than young Davenant.

'Corsa ravished, the Count / abused.'

It was not a question what would happen next but how.

'Weep no more for what is past,' sang a boy in sweet, fluting treble, not so well as Miracle had.

Foreste confronted his sister, the wronged, raped Corsa.

'Kneel and be nimble in devotion. / Thou art to die.'

Did honour really demand it? She didn't struggle as her twin tied her down into a chair.

He slit her wrists, copious liquid pouring into a basin – some clever stage trick, Palmer guessed. Sad recorders accompanied her dying in falling tones.

The rest of the play was a rush to the bitter end driven by Count Lucio returning from the front to ally himself with Foreste in getting revenge on the Duke.

When the Duke begged them to strike him down, go on, go on, Palmer mentally urged, get it over and done with....

But how? Enter the Duke's villain Castruchio and his gang to ambush all three heroes in a mêlée!

The Duke and Count Lucio fell dying to the stage.

Palmer guessed that what was coming would be wordy in the way of dying speeches.

'*Nay let us join hands. / We do forgive each other and the world.*'

Palmer swore he heard a sob from old Ralph the Librarian.

The moral of the play was solemnly intoned.

'*So intricate is Heaven's revenge 'gainst lust / the righteous suffer here, with the unjust.*'

... which was a novel way of putting it to Palmer's way of thinking.

He was on his way out when a stranger stopped him.

'Nicholas Lanier,' the man reminded him, 'Master of the King's Musick....'

Just as he had said he would be.

'... some of the musicians tonight were mine, that is, the King's.'

What could he want? Palmer asked himself.

'I believe young master D'Avenant has a future, wouldn't you agree? The question is, where?'

Wherever he could get it Palmer guessed, in the playhouse of the better kind like here in Blackfriars.

'It's London and the Court for him.'

Miracle's words in Oxford came back to him – a play, this play might well be heard at Court; there were plenty of courtiers in tonight. Was that what Lanier was suggesting?

'The masque's the present thing,' said Lanier. 'Mr Porter is of the same opinion, Mr Endymion Porter, who has the ear of the King. If I were young D'Avenant I should put my works before Porter as I write them. I might even write a poem to him – as I gather Mr Porter likes to do himself to influential friends. It guarantees they are read, and if they please that they are circulated.'

Palmer felt himself to be an unlikely channel of influence with the boy writer. What was clear was that there was no false modesty in the Court circle which Davenant, as Palmer continued to think of him, was aspiring to. It brought back to Palmer's mind another poet who had written private poetry to the great if not the good, Shakespeare to Southampton, both dead, both enshrined in print. As for Davenant's ambitions in the masques, what was it with those cursed, arse-numbing spectacles?

'I have been in Italy, to Venice,' Lanier said as if he thought Palmer would care. 'There is a Signor Monteverdi, he has gone beyond the masque to create something new.'

If that meant the masque was finished, thank God for that, thought Palmer.

'I thought you had picture business in Mantua,' he said. 'You talked about it when we last met.'

'It is going well. There too I have seen this new music. Some call it opera.'

Some who were illiterate; opera was the plural of opus meaning a work, therefore works. Palmer did not say it.

'... others say, the lyric art, from Orpheus and his lyre. It will come to England. It is composed throughout. The text is set in the form of recitative instrumentally accompanied – a sort of sung speech or chant just how we believe the Greeks used to perform their sublime drama. This takes the action forward. Any noble sentiment of love, or hate, or rage, or pity is placed in the aria, the air as we call it in England, that is, the song....'

Seeing Palmer getting a little lost in the explanation, Lanier patiently explained.

'Aria equals tune or melody, Mr Palmer. As for recitative, this new form is the true, dramatic marriage of words and music.'

'And you think that this is where young Davenant might come in?'

Lanier inclined a bow.

'Young men's heads are turned, especially young men of twenty-one as he is. If this play we have seen today does well, the King's Men will be at him for another. The opera must wait but it will come. I for one shall make it come which D'Avenant may follow. Meantime there is another *surer* route our friend might take.'

Lanier looked around, careful not to be overheard.

'... the Queen.'

The Queen?

A slip of a girl of eighteen unhappy with her husband or so it was said, with his country and most definitely with his religion. She was not even close to him. That place was reserved for George Villiers and he was busy preparing for war against her nation France.

Lanier led Palmer to a more secluded place.

'Queens enjoy their own Courts. The last Queen, Anne did, Maria – as His Majesty calls his wife – will do so too especially if the King chooses to spend his time elsewhere. Her taste is for romance, courtly love – love expressed in the game of words if you understand me; she is, will ever be the faithful wife.'

'There wasn't much that was romantic in tonight's play.'

'Oh, young William will get over all that David and Jonathan brotherly love once he has left Brooke House....'

Palmer raised an eyebrow as if to ask why?

'... because he is an artist and so he must spread his wings.'

'You think Brooke will allow it?'

'Brooke is no great favourite at Court. He is old, past his three score and ten. Time will have its way with him.'

Palmer was reminded of his own time. Sixty was beckoning.

'And you are close to the Queen?'

'I shall be, Mr Palmer, I shall be. I am high in the regard of a certain Lord and as you know....'

... this Lord had negotiated the marriage between Charles and the French princess while his Lady was the Queen's closest confidante when she wasn't looking after the desires of George Villiers, Duke of Buckingham, a man not her husband.

What webs, what webs, Palmer thought.

Nicholas Lanier left Palmer in no doubt where Davenant's future lay.

'I speak to you as an older, wiser head than young Mr D'Avenant's. It may be that I can offer him a way to the Queen even if I am the King's man – I have said as much to my cousin Henry who also has influence with young William. You, Mr Palmer, look out for Miracle and her child. Do you not think the world of the Court more salubrious for her and hers than the hurly-burly of the playhouse? Please carry that thought with you. I have a motive. I shall want another poet for my operas one of these days.'

~ 12 ~

HENRY AND JOYCE LANIER were involved with a production of their own, their first child after four years of marriage. They called her Mary, the popular name for the French Queen. Emilia insisted that the mother's lying in for this first grandchild must be in her house in Clerkenwell where the baby was duly baptised in St James's Church.

'It's time we had our own lodgings,' Miracle said to her husband, pregnant with their second child.

It could not be in Brooke House so Davenant pretended not to hear. Life there gave him the opportunity to mix with those connected with the Court. He talked frequently about Mr Endymion Porter.

'... my patron in the Court,' he grandly claimed. 'He is close to King Charles, he is a man of art and letters. And he is one of Buckingham's closest friends.'

By contrast in the Charterhouse, Palmer was defending himself against the snipings of the Preacher.

'Mr Palmer, your ways continue most irregular!'

Palmer wouldn't have cared had it not been for the shilling fines these ways of his brought down on him.

Yet they were nothing like as threatening as the year's events turned out to be.

War against Spain opened with an attack on Spanish Cadiz led by Villiers, Duke of Buckingham. It brought disgrace on the English troops – for getting drunk in the town's wine cellars instead of pressing home their assault.

Next it was carried to France.

France's fault was to ally itself secretly with Spain and to oppress its Protestant minority, the Huguenots who were holed up behind the walls of La Rochelle on the western seabord.

Villiers fitted out eighty ships to carry six thousand men in an attack on the Ile de Re off the coast from the threatened city, an island occupied by French crown forces.

Palmer received an urgent summons from Miracle.

'William hasn't gone to the wars, has he?'

This was Palmer's first thought when he found her in tears trying to attend to her child with the next one visibly on the way. Young men and their dreams of adventure....

'No, but he wanted to. You know how he is, always wanting to be in the thick of things, seeking reputation, he calls it....'

Even in the cannon's mouth? Palmer wasn't so sure.

'But he hasn't gone....'

'No but he's just written a letter to the King.'

Miracle produced a sheet of paper. Palmer read it.

What it offered was something incredibly stupid.

'He wants to blow up the enemy magazine in Dunkirk?'

How?

Palmer read on – Davenant claimed an insider friend who would infiltrate him with the aim of placing an incendiary device in the enemy magazine, a service he would perform 'even at the cost of my own life'.

As he read this Palmer broke out laughing.

'It's not funny, Godfather,' Miracle complained.

'This is playhouse stuff,' Palmer reassured her. 'Just tear it up.'

'I can't do that!'

'Then hide it. How are you for money?'

The answer was not well. Glorious dreams by William did not always include food on the table for her and the children. Palmer handed over most of what he had on him.

News of Villiers's adventure began to filter back.

Palmer knew how to read it. Heroic attacks on Saint Martin de Re? Attacks repulsed. Our brave men bearing up against adversity? No pay getting through, disease setting in.

He had seen it all before in person.

After three months the invasion force pulled out, defeated and heavily depleted. Protestant La Rochelle went unrelieved.

Were lessons learned? Not if the stories Palmer was hearing were true that Villiers was now set on a second expedition to the consternation of England's French Queen and the sympathetic fascination of a Court which had taken to speaking French, to help Henrietta Maria's little English.

'Masquers do not make soldiers, personal bravery is not enough,' Palmer said pointedly to his guest in the Bell Inn, Ralph the Librarian after telling him about the latest

Davenant flight of explosive fancy. 'How is it in Brooke House?'

The old Librarian sighed.

'The Master and I are of an age. He is in the country. He has been making his will.'

'Something in it for you, I hope?'

'Oh, I don't know. I haven't been long in his service albeit the service I have done him is of considerable worth. You cannot imagine the state the library was in, so typical of a man of letters – books everywhere and in every condition kept, or rather not kept without system or organisation, all higgledy-piggledy.'

Ralph put his hand to his mouth, embarrassed by the boldness of his statement.

'So you *are* hoping there might be something in the will for you?'

The older man looked back sadly at the younger greyhair.

'I have nowhere to go if he goes before me.'

'What! Even in these more favourable times,' here Palmer lowered his voice, 'for the Catholic faithful?'

'Her Majesty the Queen is only traduced by this sort of gossip.'

Was mild Ralph expressing annoyance?

'... if she does worship in the old faith, it is in its most modern, reasoned form.'

'Whatever can you mean?'

'There is very little difference between the higher practice of our own State's religion and French religious belief.'

'And Her Majesty does like the secular – to dance, romance....' Palmer said to provoke him further.

They were in the dog days of August, hot and airless, ideal weather for another bout of the plague if it had a mind to break out. Anyone with sense and means was away in the country.

'News, great news!'

The shout came from an excited character in the doorway, covered in riding dust.

'... Buckingham is dead, killed by one of his officers, one Felton, at the Greyhound in Portsmouth!'

Palmer looked up.

'How *dreadful!*' Ralph whispered.

The rest of the inn broke out in cheers. Buckingham had never been a popular figure.

'A health to Mr Felton!' shouted one, mug raised in salutation.

That was unlikely, Palmer told himself who had seen men hung for treason just long enough to see their bleeding heart ripped out of their chests. Feltons never ended well.

'What did he do it for, this Felton?' he shouted across to a neighbouring table once the news had spread round.

''cos the Duke was a daisy-boy!' a man sneered back.

Palmer put his finger to his lips in warning.

Maturer information brought the usual corrections to the story – Felton was no disinterested martyr, he believed the Duke had passed him over for promotion. It didn't stop him being the hero of the hour. An older faith would have made him a saint.

'I have to leave,' the old librarian said to Palmer, worried by all the drama. 'Tomorrow I go into the country, to Warwick Castle to be with my Lord now that his library here is in good order.'

Such were the obligations of service, Palmer reflected. They didn't apply to young Davenant. He had been given leave by Brooke to stay with wife and family in town provided he got down to some writing.

Fat chance of that, Palmer reckoned. And he was right. The young man was too busy going out in search of whatever company he could find left in the Capital, spending the little money he had. Miracle and the children were not foremost in his mind. Nicholas Lanier's advice, about the advantage to wife and mother being greater with a husband employed in the Court came back into Palmer's mind.

At least when the second fleet Buckingham had organised sailed out, Davenant did not sail with it.

The result was no better. The fleet withdrew, La Rochelle went unrelieved and soon surrendered.

King Charles's experiment in active foreign policy was over and done with for good.

The tug at Palmer's pensioner cloak in Chapel was vehement and repeated.

He looked up from his prayerbook to see William Davenant.

'Urgent news!' the young man whispered.

Palmer tipped his cap to the Preacher before he made his way out of the Chapel. The look of irritation on the man's face always made him feel much better.

Outside Davenant could not hold back.

'Brooke has been stabbed in Warwick Castle, he is hovering between life and death!'

Greville, Lord Brooke knifed, whatever for? He was living in retirement among his books, he wasn't a danger to anybody. Was he mixed up in the Villiers affair? The two men had never been friendly.

'Who did this?' Palmer demanded.

'That's the worry. The message was garbled. But it did say Ralph.'

Palmer was stunned.

'Ralph? Why, whatever for?'

'I have no idea. The story goes that the Master asked him to witness his will....'

Palmer imagined the scene – the will, a request to sign it, a hurried eye looking for sight of some word, gesture, provision for his old age finding none then, panic!

But murder? Who would have thought Ralph had it in him?

'Worse,' Davenant went on, 'Ralph turned the knife on himself afterwards.'

Better that than to let the Law take its awful course. Poor old men, both of them.

'I must go to him,' Davenant said, thinking of Lord Brooke.

Palmer detained him with a hand on his arm thinking of old Ralph.

'I will come with you.'

There were arrangements to be made for pregnant Miracle and her boy with Emilia and her household in Clerkenwell.

'Death of the great always brings work for us musicians,' said Henry Lanier. 'The Duke of Buckingham's funeral will be a big show.'

Palmer asked for the news from the Court.

'The King and Queen are wonderfully reconciled. It's rumoured that Her Majesty is again with child – the first was stillborn.'

Palmer was not the only one to think of the irony of Henrietta Maria made pregnant, Villiers despatched both by the hand of Fate at the very same time as if one could not have happened without the other.

'My cousin Lanier....'

Davenant sat forward with interest.

'... is to compose a lamentation on the death of the Duke.'

'And the text?' Davenant asked.

Palmer watched him closely. Hadn't he written the drama of brother spirits dying together in love?

Henry Lanier spread his hands in apology.

'He will have very little time....'

The Master of the King's Musick would want to strike while the iron was hot to please his own master.

'... so the last thing he said to me was that he will use the subject of Hero and Leander.'

Palmer wracked his brains. At last it came to mind – a youth swimming the Hellespont to seek a maiden's love. An odd simile.

'It's from classical mythology out of Ovid,' Henry Lanier confirmed. 'Nicholas says he will fashion his own text in English.'

Was there another? Oh yes, by Marlowe, a name Palmer knew only as a roisterer who got himself killed in a brawl leaving the stage free for William Shakespeare.

'Will he now?' Davenant said, disappointment spreading across his face.

Palmer was feeling his age as the pair rode westwards on the Oxford road. The exercise was not doing him any good. Everything vital ached.

Arriving in Oxford they stayed the night at the Tavern. William's sister Jane, now Hallam was friendly on the face of it.

'Let's take some wine,' William said with a wink to Palmer.

Sure enough, they were presented with a bill for it 'according to the terms of our father's will,' said Jane waiting for payment.

A second hard ride took them to the gates of Warwick Castle. Everywhere were signs of modern repair.

'Lord Brooke has made his life's work of it,' Davenant said as they passed inside.

They were not immediately admitted to Brooke's bedroom. Instead Palmer found a face he was not expecting, of Dr John Hall from nearby Stratford. Palmer took him aside.

'I know you do not talk about your patients....'

'Lord Brooke is not my patient. I came here in case I could be of some help. He is our lord and master hereabouts.'

'What is your diagnosis?'

'I am not the doctor in the case. Myself, I would have cleaned the wound and called in a surgeon to sew the gash. We cannot know if vital organs have been impaired, that is in God's care.'

'What have they done, the doctors in the case?'

Hall looked doubtful.

'They have lined the wound with mutton fat in the hope it will mend itself!'

... which was not good according to Dr Hall.

Davenant called Palmer away.

'We are permitted to see His Lordship.'

Fulke Greville, Baron Brooke lay propped up on pillows and in pain.

Palmer wrinkled his nose at the putrid smell. He had seen wounds in battle, watched them grow green and men die in agony from them. He was in no doubt this was Brooke's destiny, there was nothing Hall or any doctor could do now could save him; the rot was too far advanced.

Mutton fat!

'My boy,' Brooke said to Davenant, opening his arms.

Davenant allowed himself to be embraced despite the smell.

'Are you writing?'

Davenant nodded.

'A drama about an ancient king of the Lombards.'

The beginnings in his head not yet on the page.

'Good, good.'

'My Lord, who did this?'

Palmer was the asker. Brooke sighed.

'My manservant Ralph.'

'Your manservant?'

'Yes, he was helping me on with my breeches. He was angry about the will, my will which I had asked him to witness.'

So the motivation had been as Palmer reckoned it.

'Your manservant?' he repeated.

'Yes, Ralph Hayward. He has sadly paid the price, *felo da se*, suicide.'

'Not ... Ralph the Librarian?'

Brooke looked back in wonder before breaking out in laughter quickly throttled by pain.

'Ralph the Librarian!' he gasped. 'No, not so I assure you.'

'What do you think, Mr Palmer?'

Davenant asked the question outside the bedchamber in the presence of Dr Hall.

'I believe he will die,' Palmer said. 'Do you disagree, Dr Hall?'

Hall shook his head.

'I shall have to look for another master,' was all Davenant had to say.

Or mistress, thought Palmer, thinking of the Queen.

A frightened figure approached them, Ralph the Librarian wringing his hands.

What am I to do, the hands were saying, what *am* I to do?

'Your master will die,' Palmer said to him as gently as his nature allowed.

'What would you do, Richard?'

The use of his given name touched the old investigator.

'There is nothing for you here, Ralph. Go back to your library in Holborn and wait for the outcome of events. It will be months before any will is proved. There will be food on the table until then.'

Dr Hall intervened.

'Visit us first in Stratford – there are plenty of rooms in New Place. It is half a morning's ride away. There is nothing any of us can do here.'

Dr Hall rode ahead of them to warn his wife of the impending visit.

It was midday before the three guests, Ralph, Palmer and Davenant wheeled their horses into the grounds of the familiar manor house in the centre of the Stratford. The mistress of the house came out to greet them accompanied by her husband.

'Your daughter Elizabeth, Mrs Hall?'

Palmer had decided to have the first word.

'A married woman, Mr Palmer – Mrs Nash. Her husband Thomas, Mr Nash, he is a gentleman and a lawyer trained. They live next door.'

Hall had mentioned no grandchildren. Palmer decided not to ask. The Shakespeare clan did not appear to be particularly fecund.

The three men dismounted.

They were distributed by servants into rooms around the house, in Palmer's case to the same room where he had stayed all those years ago when he rode out in pursuit of a playwright suspected of treason. In this room a young Susanna had begged to know what would happen to her father. Neither knew then that he would die here at home in his bed.

The main meal of the day was served in the middle of the afternoon in honour of the guests after their morning ride. Dr Hall and his wife sat at opposite ends of the long oak table. A woman Palmer recognised as the daughter Elizabeth took a place alongside her mother. At the last minute a figure unknown to Palmer bustled in to take his place on Susanna's other side.

'Thomas Nash,' the man announced himself before sitting down and tucking straight into his soup.

A florid man, he was in his middle thirties Palmer judged, a good dozen years older than his wife. He plainly liked his food, cutting himself a large slab of bread to go with the pottage.

Dr Hall made the introductions. When it came to his son-in-law Palmer attempted civility.

'I understand you are a lawyer, Mr Nash.'

Nash nodded, masticating his food.

'My father Anthony was a friend and associate of Mr Shakespeare who bought this house. My uncle John owned the Bear Inn. As heir to both I was left comfortably provided – very comfortably,' he said, smiling in the direction of his wife. 'I have never needed to practise the Law.'

'Did you study in London?' Palmer asked.

Nash took a long slurp of his soup.

'Lincoln's Inn,' he said.

'They like the plays at the Inns of Court,' Ralph the Librarian turned to his hostess to suggest, 'including those by your father, Mrs Hall.'

'Can't say *I* did,' said Nash ignoring his mother-in-law. 'Of course Mr Shakespeare had retired by the time I went up, indeed he had already sadly left this mortal life. I knew him of course – he was a friend of my father as I said, but rather as ... a gentleman, a gentleman of Stratford.'

'In London he was a King's Man,' Palmer said.

'At Court,' Davenant put in.

'And at the Globe and Blackfriars Playhouses.'

Palmer could not resist the implication that it was an *ungentlemanly* trade which had made the money which paid for the imposing residence in which they were dining, property no doubt to be passed on to Nash and his wife in due course.

Nash saw it. He changed the subject.

'I gather you have come from Lord Brooke in Warwick Castle. Bad business. What brought it about?'

'A hopeful heir disappointed in his expectations,' Palmer said drily.

'Oh, I wouldn't call Haywood that,' Ralph the Librarian protested. 'He was my Lord's manservant.'

'He had expectations all the same.'

The voice was Susanna Shakespeare's.

It surprised most of the guests used to women saying nothing at table.

'Just so,' Dr Hall agreed unshocked by his wife's intervention.

Palmer looked across to Elizabeth. She kept her eyes lowered, the wife of her husband rather than a chip off the old Shakespeare block he decided.

'My husband tells me you are Jennett Davenant's son,' Susanna Shakespeare said to her youngest guest.

Did Palmer see a glint of steel in her eyes?

Davenant nodded gracefully.

'I never met her,' Mrs Shakespeare said.

'Did your father talk about her?' Davenant asked. 'He stayed as a guest of my parents in Oxford many times.'

Risky, Palmer thought, risky.

'I cannot say he did, he was often on the road between here and London. He stayed in many places as the fancy took him no doubt.'

That put the Davenants in their place. Palmer waited for the next round.

'I have heard more about your parents from my husband,' Susanna said.

Then why the 'Jennett'?

Palmer could see that young William was asking himself the same. He hoped that the boy would not be so foolish as to try any talk of paternity!

'I have the honour of following your father in his profession,' the young man said instead, causing Nash to gurgle over his spoon. 'My first play was performed by his company in the Blackfriars Theatre. Do you know it, Madam?'

'The play or the playhouse?' she asked with a hint of amusement.

Dr Hall intervened.

'My wife never goes to London. I do. My late father-in-law bought lodgings in the Blackfriars Gatehouse. I use them when I have business in London.'

'Do you attend the playhouse nearby, sir?' Davenant asked, encouraged.

Hall's smile was thin.

'I said I knew the Capital. Of course I do not go to plays.'

Nash spoke up.

'As a family we do not approve of such entertainments.'

So Shakespeare's granddaughter was married to a Puritan, Palmer told himself. Poor Elizabeth. Not that he liked the plays either but that was a matter of education and not religious proscription.

'The King and Queen enjoy them,' Davenant said, coolly and with disarming charm. 'Mr Shakespeare's plays still hold the stage.'

Nash returned a disparaging look.

'I am not convinced that Mr Shakespeare favoured performance of the plays here in Stratford. I do not remember him discussing them in my father's or my uncle's presence.'

Palmer decided to bait him.

'When I was last here, some of the King's Men told me they had been paid not to perform in the town despite being servants of the King.'

'*Quod erat demonstrandum*,' Nash retorted. 'Mr Shakespeare was known as a gentleman of this town interested in the town's affairs not as a ... a *player* in the public eye. Indeed I have heard some question the veracity of whether this trade was indeed what he practised.'

'What, as player or playwright?'

Palmer had seen the man play, he had handled copies of his printed plays, name on the title-page.

'Both. I have seen a copy of his will, Mr Palmer, there is no mention of playbooks or playhouse shares.'

So it went, Palmer thought to himself, inconvenient truths transmuted into convenient fairytales.

'What do ... these people think Mr Shakespeare was employed doing in the Capital?'

Nash waved his spoon.

'There are many employments, in the City, in the Court.'

Palmer appealed to Dr Hall.

'I told you, I do not go to the plays,' was all the Doctor would say.

But he would have seen the playbills, Palmer knew, and knew that Dr and Mrs Hall knew too.

'If Mr Nash is right,' Palmer contented himself with saying to his hosts, 'I fear you will have to change your inscription on Mr Shakespeare's memorial bust. Perhaps "wealthy in rents" would be more accurate, or "skilled in land leases". In Latin of course.'

Nash shrugged.

Davenant opened his mouth to speak. Was he going to take Nash on? Palmer asked himself. The boy knew Hemmings, co-editor of Shakespeare's plays. Other actors who had worked with Shakespeare today parroted Davenant's lines. Palmer was in for a surprise.

'The sacred drama is fit employment for a gentleman. The dowager Duchess of Richmond &

Lennox believes it so, so did Baron Brooke of Warwick Castle......'

Nash moved his head in grudging acceptance.

'... indeed a gentleman dramatist might aspire to serve the Crown, as I believe Mr Shakespeare did.'

Susanna Shakespeare spoke.

'Well, all I can say is that in matters of the Crown, they are very welcome here, servants, King or Queen, French or Scot! Is it true, Mr Davenant that French has become the language of the Court?'

The conversation settled into calmer, more trivial waters.

~ 13 ~

'SO THAT WAS MY half-sister Susanna.'

Davenant said the words to Palmer alone on horseback the next day, on their way back to London. Ralph the Librarian was dallying some paces behind on his smaller mount.

'I see no resemblance, no resemblance at all!'

'Mr Palmer! You step on my dreams!'

And the young man laughed. Palmer's question to him was more serious.

'Now that Brooke's dead, what will you do now, where will you go?'

Palmer had it mind that the lad would finally set up house with his wife and two children, William and the expected newborn.

'I shall seek the kindness of friends. For example Mr Porter....'

'... will have his own worries,' Palmer interrupted him, 'now that his patron Buckingham is food for worms just like Brooke.'

'Then I shall go to Mr Hyde. I don't think you know him – he has rooms in the Middle Temple where he is studying the Law. He has often invited me to share them,' Davenant said, 'without the burden of study.'

He laughed gaily at his own joke.

His levity was soon brought down to earth by the birth some weeks later of a daughter, another Elizabeth.

Nicholas Lanier's lamentation for the Duke of Buckingham was announced to be performed in the Palace of Whitehall. His creation interested Palmer because of its claims to follow ancient Greek performance, declaiming its drama to music 'in the recitative style'.

Palmer was a man of classical tastes. He persuaded Davenant to find a way to get him in.

'Nicholas has allowed me to help him with the text,' Davenant confided. 'Very deep, very deep.'

Entry came through Davenant's still-grieving friend Endymion Porter provided Palmer dressed in his gentleman-pensioner's cloak and sat among the lowest orders.

'I wouldn't want to sit anywhere else,' Palmer complained.

What Palmer and the audience heard went beyond anything previously known in England.

Court ears familiar with the masque might understand solo airs, part songs, choruses and the all-important music for the dance which was where royal interest really lay. Connecting musical passages and interludes such as Ferrabosco had exposed them to were already understood.

What they had never heard was the concerting of words and music throughout in a single narrative.

Lanier's clear, bright tenor touched higher notes before falling lower into the richest part of his voice. His vocal line was accompanied by his lute to which it was his habit to compose. A small stringed consort introduced and concluded the scene – Palmer was pleased to see Henry Lanier its chief viol player.

The erotic story of lust-struck athletic youth swimming a watery gulf to reach a submissive maiden with its sex-as-death theme made famous by Ovid and then Marlowe had been concentrated into one episode. Maiden Hero panted and pined in Lanier's sweetest voice as she waited in doubt and torment for Leander to appear for their promised tryst.

Nor com'st thou yet, my slothful love, nor yet.

The encounter did not appear to strike the listeners as uncomfortable applied to the friendship of Charles and Buckingham. Charles as the expectant Hero, Buckingham as the indefatigable Leander? Palmer asked himself. Only he wasn't, indefatigable in war and now in death, he was another one turning to dust, dead just as Leander had died too, drowned on the return swim!

Lanier – with Davenant's help, Palmer wondered from what the young man had told him – telescoped this death into the report of the waiting Hero. This was as it should be, Palmer approved, not like Shakespeare killing his Romeo and Juliet in plain sight against all traditions of antiquity.

Woe's me, 'tis he, drowned by the impetuous floods.... To thee I come. Leander's bosom shall be Hero's tomb.

At this the King, standing close to the singer, so close that he rested his hand on Lanier's shoulders as he was singing, appeared to start forward as if anxious to join the love figure in death himself. And his Queen looked on with what Palmer could only describe as remarkable sympathy.

What remained with Palmer was the singer's plea.

... spare, o spare my jewel; pity the cries and tears of wretched Hero.

'I am to be presented to the King and Queen!'

Davenant's excitement was palpable.

'... they are receiving guests in the royal apartments. Mr Lanier has arranged it – Mr Nicholas. He says I am to look to charm the Queen especially.'

Palmer shrugged.

'When is this to happen?'

'Now. Fortunately I am wearing my best suit, tailor Urswick's finest. Will you come with me?'

Palmer was surprised.

'Why me? I shall only look out of place. They might not let me past the door.'

'Well, you are my guardian in a kind of way.'

Davenant prepared Palmer as best he could on their way through guarded door after door to their royal destination.

'Since Villiers's death the royal couple have become especially close, so Nicholas tells me. Of course it helps that she is with child but there is something more.'

Palmer asked what it was.

'She showed great understanding about Villiers and what he meant to her husband the King.'

What did he mean to the King? Palmer asked himself.

There was a scurrilous answer, the same that Villiers had meant to old King James who had called him 'wifey'. On the other hand Villiers's rise had gone hand in hand with Charles's as if the royal Prince had attached himself to the favourite rather than the other way round, beginning when Villiers had persuaded Charles to lead the masque-dancing as a way of growing closer to his father, the old King. James had loved watching the dance, especially when danced by androgynous youth.

Perhaps it was better to leave the question wrapped up in the purer beauty of the music and words they had all heard today. Life rarely emulated art, it was altogether messier.

'Were Charles and James not close?' Palmer asked.

'Not especially. My friend Porter tells me that His Majesty was, other than in his love of books and art, a disappointment to his father. Small, sickly....'

Unlike the dead Prince, the elder brother Henry who had been everything a royal Prince ought to be and Charles was not. Perhaps Villiers had been the Henry substitute, the older brother to a young Prince Charles, a closer, kinder one too, one who would encourage him in life rather than present an impossible model for emulation in death. But now Villiers was dead too.

The gathering in the royal apartments was select, dozens of courtiers rather than hundreds. Gaps in their ranks from time to time allowed Palmer to see what was going on in the heart of the party.

The Queen lay reclined on a couch plumped up with cushions as befitted her pregnant condition. She was attended by a better-looking woman, her new confidante Palmer presumed, wife of the Lord who had fixed the royal marriage, mistress of the late Buckingham. What was going through her mind, not only Palmer was wondering. Room in front of the women allowed favoured people to be presented to Her Majesty and her graceful hand which she offered to be kissed.

Further away but not too far stood the tiny King surrounded by an outer ring of gentlemen of the bedchamber, once again with space to allow the chosen to come and go. At present it was occupied by Nicholas Lanier, the day's performer.

'We ... shall hear the work again, Master Lanier, and again,' the King was saying to his musician. 'The ... love of Hero for Leander, she for ... him and he for ... her, is from Ovid of course....'

That the King came close to stammering, Palmer heard for the first time.

Lanier was busy bowing his agreement at such spectacular royal knowledge. There was more to come.

'... written in our language originally by this, this Marlowe ... whom ... we do not know, other than in his plays we have ... seen or read, and that ... rarely.'

'Your Majesty is wonderfully well-informed,' Lanier was heard by all to say.

'We read, Master Lanier, we read and we, we, we ... enjoy the plays. But our preference is Mr ... Shakespeare

– not the tumbledown ... bawdy stuff of course. We have in our library his Folio much read *and* annotated by our royal hand....'

So one of Jaggard's great books, fixed up by Palmer had found a royal home, the old investigator was almost pleased to hear. The royal voice lisped on.

'It is our custom to write down the main ... matter or the character who impresses us ... most.'

'Would Your Majesty favour us with an example?'

Ha! That put him on the spot thought Palmer, well done Lanier.

The King appeared only too ready.

'*Much ... Ado About ... Nothing*; can anyone tell me the story of that play?'

No-one could or thought it unwise to anticipate the King's knowledge.

'I call it Benedick and ... Beatrice for theirs are the characters who are at the heart of the play, who most, who most engage our ... hearts.'

Polite wonder greeted this assessment.

'Let us ... try you again. *Twelfth ... Night*?'

'Surely sire, Malvolio?' a voice chirped up.

Palmer recognised its owner, the bucolic Mr Endymion Porter, the Prince's go-to man on culture and early taster of Davenant's playwriting talent in Ely House.

The King did not look entirely pleased.

'Yes indeed. "*Some ... are born to greatness, some .... achieve greatness, and some ... have greatness thrust upon 'em.*"'

Nobody risked making a faux pas as to where His Majesty might place himself – the first, correct; the second, only in the flattery of the masques; and as for the third, only too true given the death of Prince Henry. A man might be easily misunderstood in making any comment, even Palmer understood that.

'*All's ... Well That Ends ... Well*? You will not find that one so easy....'

No-one did.

'It's a rare ... play not often seen if ever. Parolles, I call it, for the ... braggart who patrols the play with ... fantastic eff-, eff-, effrontery not, alas, matched by his courage. Ah, Mr ... Shakespeare!'

'"*Thou should'st be living at this time*",' quoted the undeterred Endymion Porter.

'Yet why, why, why ... speak of artists dead when we have before us one who is so very much alive? An ornament in the seeing and the ... hearing is so much more to be ... prized than one in the telling.'

The King looked up benevolently at the day's performer.

Lanier's bow was even lower this time. He took his cue and backed away.

'*Stand not on the order of your going*' came into Palmer's mind from somewhere or other. There would doubtless be a handsome prize in the form of a bulging royal purse waiting for the musician on his way out. So he was surprised to see Lanier making his way towards him and Davenant instead.

Lanier spoke directly to the younger man.

'How is your French? We must present you to Her Majesty.'

Davenant was too young and ambitious to admit 'so-so'.

'What should I talk about to recommend myself?' he asked Lanier. 'Might I dedicate my next play to her or suggest that the next will be a romance? You told me that Her Majesty likes romances.'

'If it's in a language she can understand. As for making dedications, too near the sun for the present, dear boy – find some high-placed nobleman or other as your first step, it's the usual way.'

Davenant's question remained open.

'Let her see you,' Lanier decided, 'let her know you wish to be of service to her in some *courtly* entertainment which will please her and her ladies.'

'A masque?'

'If so let her suggest it.'

Lanier began to lead Davenant away in another royal direction. His eyes told Palmer to stay where he was. Palmer understood. There was no need for an old Adam in the picture.

The level of conversation had become such that Palmer could not hear what was being said when at last Davenant got his turn before the Queen. It was like watching one of the old dumb shows where characters mimed the events about to unfold in the play.

The Queen presented her gloved hand, jewelled all the same. Palmer watched Davenant bow gracefully, not too little not too much to brush it with his lips. The Queen spoke. Davenant smiled. The second time she spoke he laughed, an attractive laugh, good teeth (which could not be said of the Queen's little protuberances). Lanier intervened – something Davenant had not understood or could not express? Davenant's hand touched his heart – a royal promise received? Lanier moved him gently away before he was ready to go, the only false step by the younger man but one which the Queen appeared to find endearing as she cast a remark upwards from behind her fan to her confidante, a witty remark because the Lady laughed, her eyes following the young man with approval.

A quietly excited Davenant returned to Palmer.

'Her Majesty *hopes* that I will one day write for the Court and if I do, that it should be in a style she will enjoy. She appreciates that His Majesty has great taste in the arts and she admires them too, in a less *English* way.'

'Mais moins dans la mode anglaise....'

Palmer heard Davenant repeating the phrase to himself all the way out of the royal palace.

~ 14 ~

T HE TIME LEADING UP to the change of the decade into the 1630s witnessed England, having overspent itself in men and treasure in war against Spain and France, make a hurried peace with each and withdraw from continental politics.

Queenly hints to Davenant did not translate into hard prospects. His *Lombard* play was not staged. He had the wit instead to get out and about among the wits at Court.

'My day will come soon,' he promised his wife Miracle in their mean lodgings among a growing family he did his best to provide for. Publication of the unstaged play brought in much-needed pounds along with a couple of other pieces which did not hold the stage for long.

'I am learning,' Davenant told his friends. 'A writer must spend twice the time cutting and polishing as he does on the initial creation.'

In Clerkenwell Henry and Joyce Lanier had a growing family to look after as well which kept Emilia busy. Henry was doing well in Court music under his cousin Nicholas. A son was born to him and his wife Joyce in the depth of midwinter and baptised Henry in St James's Church.

'Named after his father,' the proud mother said.

And also after his presumed grandfather if Emilia had anything to do with it, Palmer reckoned, trying to stay warm under his cloak in the frigid church building, sympathising with the swaddled child as ice-cold water touched his forehead. Emilia would have insisted on the name Henry for the noble blood of grandad Hunsdon or Southampton, whichever she fancied it was.

She wasn't going to have a plain William.

Otherwise all Palmer saw was a regular changing of the guard. Well ensconced in the Charterhouse he was moving up into the senior ranks of the gentlemen – pensioners as Time cut its way through their numbers. Reduced means kept him in more. He made it a point not to be difficult in his domestic arrangements so he was regular in his attendance at meals in the Great Hall. He had fewer excuses these days to absent himself from church or the money to pay the fines in lieu.

'No longer Gadabout Palmer?' the Preacher challenged him one day.

There were compensations. The introduction of a fine organ into the chapel lightened the weight of the religious wordery in the daily services and lent some counterpoint to the oratundity of the Preacher. The Great Chamber sometimes staged entertainments. When it did, Palmer let his eye wander over the fine fireplace and among the tapestries like the Queen of Sheba visiting King Solomon. On the plaster ceiling he admired the purple thistles symbolically commissioned by a previous owner, the Howard duke, unwisely so since he had lost his head for plotting unsuccessfully with Mary, Queen of Scots against Elizabeth. His thoughts turned to another Howard more than Davenant's ever did, the Double Duchess who had started her third widowhood by occupying herself with the commission of a magnificent tomb in Westminster Abbey to the late Duke. There were to be no more husbands now that old King James was dead.

The ambition of men and women, Palmer told himself who'd had little of his own other than survival. His highest stakes these days were food on the table and a roof over his head.

The room reminded him of its equal in the Palace of Whitehall. There he had seen things in his time, old Queen Elizabeth the night before her favourite Essex's execution played to by the man Shakespeare and his co-mates in order to cheer her up and to save the actors' skins for their own complicity in the affair; or King James playing conciliator onstage between the rival houses of Montague and Capulet when Palmer had thrown Ben Jonson out of the audience for bad behaviour.

All gone now he reflected, both monarchs, Shakespeare, Burbage king of the actors, Richard Field the publisher of his friend Shakespeare and Jaggard, son and father both, publishers of the Stratford man's posterity in his collected plays; more recently Condell who had helped him with old Hemmings.

He'd heard that Hemmings was ill. Who was left? Burbage's brother, Cuthbert the man of business arguing with the new generation who wanted shares in the lucrative playhouse business. Fat old Ben Jonson, he was still around albeit in decline, continuing to quarrel with his partner Inigo Jones, waiting for his Mastership of the Revels except that the present incumbent Herbert was a comparative stripling.

'There's always hope for a new plague,' Palmer imagined Jonson joking.

A new arrival in the Charterhouse brought Palmer some lighter relief.

'Captain Hume,' the man introduced himself in a light Scots brogue, 'Tobias Hume.'

Hume was a tale-teller Palmer quickly found out, of his time in the Scottish Court when James was its King – 'he could'na get himself down to London quick enough!' – and of his soldiering days in the frozen north fighting for the Swedes and the Russians – 'I could'na wait to get myself home to the sunshine of Edinburgh, let me tell ye.'

Music was their first introduction.

'Masters Tallis and Byrd this morning,' Hume had said as he took a place unintroduced alongside Palmer while the new organist played introits. 'Papists both which did'na bother Queen nor King so long as they wrote them their royal music.'

He revealed himself to be a talented musician.

'Composer and *publishea*, ma friend.'

Palmer was surprised to be called friend by anyone. Hume gave him the background.

'I am, or was a viol-player, an instrument much superior to the lute. I had ma arguments with dismal Dowland over that I'll tell ye.'

He was a joker, one who was quite determined to speak loudly in order to be heard and so Palmer's replacement as the number one troublemaker in the Preacher's eyes. As a Scots chancer who had come south under James Stuart, he was the type Palmer expected to hate but he could not. Somehow – Palmer could not fathom how – Hume was a man who rarely made enemies whatever he got up to.

He confided a worry he had to his new acquaintance. It was about Ralph the Librarian.

'The Brooke heir has no place for him. All he has is his pension – shillings and pence – on quarter-day.'

'Can we no' bring him in here?' Hume demanded. 'He'd be among the few who'd enjoy it!'

Palmer explained the religious objection.

Hume sucked on his habitual pipe of tobacco.

'Ye say he is still in Brooke house, waiting to be turfed oot? And he runs the library? And old Brooke, he was a collector, was he no'?'

Palmer began to realise where Hume's thoughts might be running.

'Does this Rafe, does he have the inventory?'

Palmer didn't doubt that he did.

'Has he shared it with onyone?'

Palmer began to feel uncomfortable; he could only imagine how Ralph would react to any suggestion of stealing from his old master. That servants made a national sport of robbing their masters would be no justification to the old official who had once loyally served a Chief Minister, dead Robert Cecil and kept his most secret confidences in return for a pittance.

'Way I look at it,' Hume said, puffing away, 'old Brooke would ha' wanted him looked after. It's an oversight that he has'na. And what did this ... Rafe do for him? Saved his books for him. Now I'm no' saying he should sell the whole library – the heir would see it – but a few choice pieces, books which would likely no' be read, no' be missed ... d'ye know any buyers?'

Trouble was those buyers Palmer knew in the inky world of books and publishers had gone the way of all flesh too. He couldn't believe that he was taking Hume's scheme seriously. Every time he saw the man, Hume had an extra idea to add.

'If this ... Rafe will'na help ye, ye'll have to gain entry yourself to find candidates for sale. Whatever happens the inventory must disappear. If it does no-one will be any the wiser.'

Palmer paid a visit to Brooke House half in the hope that the practicalities would rule the scheme out. He found Ralph in the library fretting about his imminent departure. Pretending to take his mind off it Palmer asked him which were the finest books in the room.

'Which one is not,' Ralph replied, 'whether for history, religion, philosophy, poetry, even plays.'

Palmer pressed him harder.

'If I were a serious collector, which would most interest me?'

Ralph gave Palmer a sideways 'what are you up to?' look.

'As a collector one would look for rarity, so the earliest editions.'

'Show me some examples,' Palmer said.

'Sidney here ... Lord Brooke loved the poetry of Philip Sidney.'

Palmer bet he did. Hadn't he been told that Brooke and Mary Sidney had quarrelled over who the curator of the poet's memory should be?

Ralph showed him early editions, multiple manuscript copies of the same works, the poet's *Apology for Poetry*, a sonnet sequence called *Astrophel and Stella* and a printed prose romance, *Arcadia*. Palmer asked to view them more closely. Some he saw were bound in covers with the Greville/Brooke arms, some had inscriptions on them and some were entirely unmarked.

These interested him the most.

It was the same when they looked at several editions of Spenser's *Faerie Queen*. Erasmus and Thomas More were well represented which pleased the ironical strain in Palmer – More had spent time in the Charterhouse pondering a religious vocation before choosing the lucre, sorry, the responsibility of the Law. Authors such as Hakluyt, Puttenham and Gascoyne were pulled out to be shown to him. Collections of prose and verse in French and Italian vied with translations of Greek and Roman classics by North and others. Bibles of all sorts going back to Tyndale detained them for more than a while – men had once risked dying for owning them, Palmer said to Ralph who tutted a Catholic apologist's equivocation.

Shyly Ralph produced a final slim volume.

'One of the first copies of *Venus & Adonis*,' he said.

'Master Shakespeare's firstborn....'

Palmer turned the pages over.

'When do you leave?' he asked the Librarian.

Ralph gave him the date.

'I shall go back into lodgings where I was before.'

Palmer didn't care to ask or know or even to imagine them.

'I shall help you on the day,' he said.

Ralph's reaction was one of surprise.

'I have ... little to take with me.'

'I'll come all the same. Don't worry, I shan't take you to your lodgings, we can have a drink in the Bell Inn for old time's sake.'

Ralph's eyes moistened.

'Do you buy precious things?'

The Deptford chandler looked back curiously at Palmer and his question.

'It depends. Precious metals do you mean, gold, silver? Or jewellery?'

'None of those. Books, rare books.'

Palmer cast his eye to the corner of the room where books were shelved, as many as he remembered from his first visit.

'Which rare books?'

Palmer drew out a list he had drawn up after his visit to Ely house.

'And these books are yours Mr Palmer?'

Palmer feigned a smile.

'I have a procurer who sells them to me, he does not know who I sell them to.'

'He *sells* them to you, does he?'

Palmer avoided the question with another.

'Perhaps you have clients who are interested in such things?'

'Perhaps. Mr Palmer but I know you live close to the limits of the Law. You will understand that a man of my sort cannot.'

'I understand.'

'Here is your list back....'

Palmer began to feel disappointed.

'Mark the books I shall tell you,' the man said.

Palmer returned to Ely house on the due date. He found Ralph where he expected in the library.

'A sad day, Richard.'

Palmer agreed.

'Time for you to have one last look in your room,' he told Ralph.

'It's really not necessary.'

'Look, I don't want to get halfway down the road with you and find you've left something behind. Humour me and while you're at it, visit the jakes – I know all about you and your bladder.'

'Perhaps it would be wise.'

Once Ralph was out of the room Palmer moved quickly. He produced a tote bag from under his black brother's cloak. Into it went a score of books chosen for lightness, rarity and unidentifiability of ownership. Listening out carefully for anyone coming he moved quickly to the one desk in the room. Its drawer was unlocked. In it he found what he was looking for, Ralph's inventory. What the heir did not know existed would not be missed. He threw it into the bag.

A key sitting on the table fitted the library door. Palmer locked it as he left and hid the key elsewhere, somewhere it could be found but not just yet.

He went to find the porter, the books in the bag masked under his cloak.

'Please tell Ralph I couldn't stay and that I will meet him later this evening in our usual inn.'

The porter asked him at what time. Palmer gave him one.

He reached the threshold of the house.

He felt a hand on his shoulder. Slowly, reluctantly he turned round.

'You the gen'l'man from the Charterhouse?' the porter asked.

Palmer said he was.

'I won't forget to tell 'im,' said the porter.

Palmer was not alone when he met Ralph in the Bell Inn. Captain Hume was with him.

'All well?' Palmer asked the new exile from Brooke House.

'Yes. I'm sorry you had to hurry off. Strange thing was, when I tried to take a last look at the library it was locked. Perhaps it was just as well.'

'Perhaps it was.'

Palmer introduced Hume before calling for more beer and a cup of his favourite sack for the ex-Librarian.

'So what will you do now?' Palmer asked his guest.

Ralph smiled apologetically.

'As I did before. But this time, I can rely on my pension thanks to the efforts of Lord Brooke.'

'Yes, thanks to Lord Brooke,' Palmer echoed him, thinking of the pension's inadequate shillings and pence. 'Captain Hume here has something to say to you.'

'Ah yes, yes indeed.'

Hume cleared his throat.

'Mr Palmer will no' have said, leastwise I hope he has'na....'

Ralph looked mystified. Hume leaned across to touch Ralph's sleeve.

'I have maself been of some service to the State of which I may no' speak,' he said, waving any question from Ralph aside. 'King James knew me, aye, he valued me. There are those, those I may no' speak of, ye ken me?' he said, tapping his nose. 'They trust ma judgement, yes they do. Where ye see examples of loyal service, Toby, they say, be pleased to recognise it on oor behalf.'

'How, recognise it?'

Hume passed over a purse, careful that no-one should see him doing it. News of money doing the rounds in the hands of the unwary had a habit of reaching the ears of nips and cutpurses.

'Inside ye will find nine gold pieces – Chrissake man, dinna open it here! Nine poonds,' he whispered.

'Nine ... pounds? That's enough to....'

'To do a lot of things,' said Palmer, 'to rent somewhere pleasant to live for a start, with money left over.'

'I must think about that,' Ralph said, half-mystified.

'Don't think too long. We'll take you to a goldsmith where the money can be kept safe.'

'So I have been remembered....'

Ralph's voice sounded wistful.

'Ye have so,' Hume cried out, slapping him on the back. 'Now, who's for another drink?'

Ralph stopped him.

'Gentlemen, today is quarter-day. I have my pension. The drinks are ... on me.'

~ 15 ~

THE NATION REJOICED at the birth of an heir to the Throne baptised Charles like his father. Some in the nation wondered what the infant's religion would be, his mother being Catholic. In London its new Bishop, Laud was encouraging a liturgical practice whose high church richness irritated the plainer Puritan faction. They smelled Popery and resented the King's active support of it.

For one coming into the world another went out, old John Hemmings.

Palmer went uninvited to his funeral in St Mary's, Aldermanbury. It was a reason to escape the Charterhouse. It was also out of bloody-minded curiosity.

The Hemmings family was large – nine children and plenty of grandchildren. As for old John about to be buried, he was apparently a model citizen and grocer according to the officiating priest! There was nothing said about his stage activities. All was to be solemn respectability in the Hemmings story, like Thomas Nash's version of William Shakespeare's in Stratford.

Palmer looked around for other evidence of the playhouse life. If there were actors there he didn't recognise them, they were after his time. He had half-expected Ben Jonson to be in attendance. The other half told him Jonson would think he had better things to do than to waste his time on a has-been in every sense of the word.

He was surprised to spot William Davenant. Davenant was surprised to see him. Palmer did not think he looked healthy when the boy came over to him; his face was marked with pocks.

'Hemmings was good to me as far back as my Oxford days,' Davenant explained himself. 'He had my *Cruel Brother* put on, don't forget. He was also helping me back into the Blackfriars which was not going down well with the writers already there.'

'What's the matter with them?'

'It's all to do with what Her Majesty told me, that night – you remember?'

Palmer remembered the occasion but not what was said.

'The new sensibility is for wit, poetry and above all, romance. I and others favoured by the Court, we are that new spirit. Hemmings saw it, he wanted us to have our chance, but as I say, the resident writers won't have us. They are still banging on with their common satires and their revenge plays. It will be war between us, that's if we are permitted to enter the field.'

War? Palmer had seen war in all its ugliness. War was not a word to apply to quarrels among scribblers.

'What field?' he asked.

'Why, the Blackfriars. Let the audiences decide! The Court will support us, writers like me, Endymion Porter will see to that – he has influence. The better class will come to our plays. We shall be the new force for a new more refined entertainment.'

Palmer changed the subject.

'What's the matter with your skin? Nothing contagious I hope.'

Davenant blushed, brushing his nose, the most affected part, with his hand.

'Too much burning the candles at both ends – working, always working.'

When Palmer next saw Davenant a few weeks later, far from clearing the nose appeared to be worse and suppurating. It was being eaten into. The Davenant proboscis was sinking lower.

He discussed his suspicions with Captain Hume.

'It's the pox, aye, the French disease,' the Captain said. 'Come on, man, I've had it, ye've had it, any man of sportive blood has. A night with Venus and Mercury for life, remember.'

Palmer did – the sweating baths with or without the mercury-based ointment. Mercury killed as well as cured, men knew that, it poisoned the blood, rotted the teeth, ulcerated the mouth. Poison was the medical answer to this infection, poison fighting poison.

'Ye'll have to speak frankly wi' him,' Hume said.

Palmer knew as much only it was difficult. Davenant was married to Miracle, Miracle was Palmer's goddaughter. Thoughts for her made up his mind. He went in search of Davenant.

'I'm not here to moralise, William, you're not the first and you won't be the last if it's what I think it is. You must seek treatment.'

Palmer wondered what the good Dr Hall would have prescribed – cleansing potions and ointment accompanied by a pursing of his lips. The young man, he noticed was already masking his face with his hand when engaging in conversation. He appeared relieved to be able to admit the condition.

'My good friend Porter has recommended me to Dr Cademan who is Her Majesty's physician. He advises the usual treatment, quicksilver with kinder remedies to follow after. I will follow his advice. I am also thinking of going into the country for the seclusion.'

'For medical reasons?'

'Not so much. My enemies – and a man of fashion is bound to have enemies – have been making fun of me, my ... nose and such. '

'It's how people are, William.'

'No, no,' said Davenant, breaking into laughter. 'I mean why must disease follow pleasure? A man will get it from a tuppenny whore, that's plain but he might also contract it from a woman of rank.'

It sounded to Palmer as if it could have been either/or although the betting he had heard was on 'dark Lucy' from Ax Yard.

'Breasts the size of the Trossachs and buttocks built to bestride a colossus.'

Hume had appeared to know what he was talking about.

'Some are born with it,' Davenant went on, 'the sins of the fathers visited on the sons. What have they done to deserve it or to pass it on?'

'Do you accuse Miracle?'

'No, no, it's me sure enough. Where there is temptation a man such as me will fall.'

'And Miracle?'

Palmer left the rest of the enquiry unsaid.

'I don't know, I don't think so, she hasn't said.'

Davenant laughed again.

'We are old marrieds, young as we are. Miracle lives for our children, I am out and about in the town morning – no, rarely in the morning, by noon certainly and at night without question. Marital congress has fewer opportunities than you might think.'

So Palmer had heard and was in this case thankful.

Palmer knew an attorney's messenger when he saw one, lurking in the Master's Court when he came out from morning chapel in the Charterhouse. Instinctively he pushed his hands into his pockets in case the man was about to try to lay a summons on him. What he got instead was an invitation to the Middle Temple 'to learn something which might be of advantage to you'.

As he walked down Chancery Lane and across Fleet Street into the legal district, memories piled on memories of dry-as-dust times spent studying under a great master of the Law, Lambarde and their strange re-encounter when the playwright Shakespeare was in trouble after the Essex rebellion. Lambarde had liked the plays. What would he have made of the plays of William Davenant, Palmer wondered? More disturbing back in the day had been chancing on Emilia Lanier in the dead of night and the events which had followed.

The attorney he met was acting for the estate of Ralph the Librarian, he said. The news came as a surprise to Palmer bringing an unwelcome sadness. Another one down.

'He has left a gift in his will, money to buy you a golden memorial ring. Forty shillings.'

Palmer took the amount in his stride.

'When, how did he die,' he asked.

'Peacefully, of old age and in the faith,' the lawyer replied, keeping his voice down.

Palmer signed a receipt for the legacy which was paid to him pedantically in forty silver shilling pieces. He sensed a pricking of his tastebuds calling him to the Bell Inn, Carter Lane last visited months ago. The least he could do was to raise a mug to his one-time friend and drinking guest there.

Outside the inn an unexpected sight brought him up short.

'Oy, Davenant!'

The figure turned and then hurried away. Palmer thrust his ancient legs forward in a determined attempt to catch up helped by the fugitive colliding with a lawyer, tipping a pile of papers onto the ground. Being Davenant, he felt obliged to help pick them up.

'Ah, Mr Palmer, I didn't see you, what are you doing here?'

Palmer kept his windfall to himself. Davenant reminded him that he was sharing rooms with a friend, Hyde. He appeared to have recovered from his illness apart from the sunken state of his nose.

'I shall still be going into the country,' he told Palmer.

Palmer didn't need to ask why – young men like Davenant had debts. His tailor Urswick, it was rumoured was busy chasing him round town with summonses, his physician Cademan went unpaid. Davenant took the not uncommon view among young gentlemen about town that credit was eternal and inextinguishable.

Palmer asked where he would go.

'My brother Robert has his parish in Wiltshire, my friend Mr Endymion Porter asks me to open up his country home in the Cotswolds and there is always my sister Jane in the old Tavern in Oxford.'

So, out west, Palmer recorded.

'Does Miracle go with you?'

Davenant looked embarrassed. He spread his hands in apology.

'We have the children to consider. And she would be so *bored*. All our countryfolk talk of is their cows and their sheep and their dairy-churnings into butter and cheese, their ailments and their jellies for good health and the lint pills they stuff into their hollow teeth. I'll be lucky if my arse sees anything better than a three-legged stool. As for entertainment the top of my hopes is for a frisky dance in a low parlour to the squeaking sound of a single fiddle. Miracle would *hate* it.'

'Have you asked her?'

Davenant spread his hands again.

'I know my wife. Mr Palmer, if it weren't for my promises to family and friends nothing could drag me away from town. Please do remember, though it grieves me to say it, my family has never entirely approved of my marriage. I see no virtue in forcing their sourpusses onto my poor wife.'

~ 16 ~

ETWEEN DAVENANT'S say and do, months passed
before he made a move.

Palmer consoled himself on the proceeds of
Ralph's legacy in beer rather than precious metal. Toby
Hume showed no signs of quitting the Charterhouse and
while he did Palmer could take any number of the deaths
of his fellow brothers in the place. It became for him his
universe as his three score and ten hoved into sight. A
husky lack of breath when he walked any distance kept
him within its scope or inside the parish of St James's in
Clerkenwell where Emilia lived on as matriarch of the
Lanier family.

Miracle came to see him with her brood. It was rare
for the Charterhouse to echo to the sounds of children.
Captain Hume entertained the pair of infants with tricks
to give Palmer time with Miracle alone.

She looked worn out, he observed, older than her
age. Her clothes were neat and clean but patched and
mended, her pale red hair which held its colour
emphasised the unnatural wanness of her skin. Bags
under her eyes and wrinkles round her mouth turned her
face downwards into disappointment more suited to an
older woman. He tried to remember her as the young
woman he had rescued in Oxford a decade ago. Life with
the mercurial, mercurious Davenant had marked her.

'I have word from William, that he is spending much
more time writing,' she said. 'Poetry now calls him he
says, there's more to writing than plays.'

Palmer asked her about money. Miracle averted her eyes.

Her godfather produced all that he could afford, ten shillings, half of what remained from Ralph's half-spent legacy. He'd had the shillings changed into a golden angel to remind Miracle of past times.

She smiled when she saw it and understood. She made no pretence of not accepting it.

The embrace she pressed on him felt ominous.

The loss was not Miracle as it turned out, but her daughter, little Elizabeth in the midwinter freeze.

Palmer saw no sign of the grieving father when he attended the funeral. The sight which affected him most was the ridiculous size of the coffin. Coffins were for the fully grown, surely, not this little casket for a baby girl carried without burden on Henry Lanier's shoulder into the church.

He did not ask for news of the absent father, he was not given any.

Two years passed until another omen of loss.

'My son is on his deathbed.'

Palmer blinked in shock when Emilia Lanier told him. He knew that it must be something grave when she came to see him in the Charterhouse. He asked her, was she sure?

'It's the dropsy,' she said, resigned.

Palmer knew the symptoms, a swelling of the limbs and a failing of the heart, an illness of the elderly he had always thought.

'How old is Henry?' Palmer asked.

'Not yet forty,' said Emilia. 'He is asking for you in the absence of his father ... who he never cared for, who never cared for him.'

Palmer agreed to go without reservation other than that he did not know what he could do to help. There would be Henry's widow and children to consider. He hadn't the means and he doubted whether Emilia was any better-placed. Joyce Lanier would be entitled to her widow's portion from her husband's estate assuming Henry had husbanded her dowry well. The Mansfields and the Laniers and the Bassanos might bear some goodwill to the family left behind but they would have responsibilities of their own.

Where would this leave Emilia?

Palmer asked her as much. Emilia took a deep breath and drew herself up to her full height.

'I must think of Henry's children,' she said.

Henry was a Court servant, his father had once enjoyed a Government perk passed onto a brother who had not shared it as he should.

'I shall fight for a pension from His Majesty!'

Emilia's eyes flashed.

Palmer did not want to be anyone however high and mighty who stood in her way!

'It is kind of you to come.'

Henry Lanier sat propped up in the only chair in the house.

'It helps drive the water down to the limbs,' he explained.

Palmer asked about his medical treatment.

'There's no cure,' Lanier said. 'The barber can let off the liquid but there's no cure for the heart.'

He took time to gather his breath.

'I've sent away the quacks, the ones who come calling with their lotions and their potions and their spells and their disgusting concoctions. It's a waste....'

And it was a waste, Palmer thought sadly, looking at the failing body in front of him.

'What can I do for you?' he asked.

'Be one of my executors.'

Palmer thought for several moments.

'Surely that is for your wife to do, or if not for your mother.'

Lanier smiled.

'Joyce is a gentle soul, it's why I married her. Mother is not! You were my go-between before....'

'I was.'

'Be so again. What Joyce is due from me has been protected, the money is safely deposited.'

Lanier gave Palmer the name of a respected goldsmith.

'And there are sufficient funds for legacies to my children when they marry or come of age. My will has been made out. Oversee it, Mr Palmer, please?'

'I am not young, Henry.'

'I think I shall die before you do.'

Lanier's joke was black.

'What about your cousin Nicholas? He *is* Master of the King's Musick.'

'Nicholas is a very busy man. He has....' and here Henry stopped to gather breath, 'he has promised to keep an eye out for my children. There are difficulties, Mr Palmer, family difficulties. My mother is determined to go to war ... I mean the Law – same thing – over my father's lost sinecure. It will mean taking on my Uncle Clement to whom it was passed.'

Palmer understood. Nicholas Lanier needed to be kept free of the family dramas Emilia was set on creating as much as she needed freedom of action herself.

'What future do you wish for your children?' Palmer asked the dying man.

Lanier smiled.

'Not the one my mother will be dreaming,' he said. 'If the boy Henry has musical talent Nicholas will make sure that it is best used. As for the girl Mary....'

A decent marriage, Palmer guessed, though what could be managed for her without a serious dowry ... it would be after his time he reckoned with relief, at least ten years away.

Lanier reached out to clasp Palmer's hand.

'I will do what you ask,' Palmer said.

'Then live a while longer, Mr Palmer....'

'Ashes to ashes, dust to dust....'

Henry Lanier's burial was a small affair. The widow and her children of six and three were taken away by her

Mansfield relatives to spare her the grief of returning to the Clerkenwell home for the time being.

Palmer found Emilia on her own in her house. She was bearing her fierce, defiant, alone-against-the-world face.

They were all gone, he realised – her sole surviving child, the husband who had abused her, all the lovers of her heyday, her lady patroness, her stinking astrologer.

'You're all that's left,' she said as if she had read his mind, in a harsh unforgiving voice.

'You have your grandchildren.'

She laughed bitterly, as if to say, and will they be spared?

'Joyce is young enough to remarry,' she said. 'Or there's talk of going away to a new life in the New World.'

The Americas?

Palmer was surprised. It was no more than a couple of tenuous footholds on a vast, inhospitable continent whatever playhouse romances of Indian princesses and handsome settlers might make pretend. It was also a haven for religious dissidents. Were Henry and his children Puritans? Palmer doubted it unless it was so on the Mansfield side.

'What will you do now?' Palmer asked Emilia.

She sighed.

'Do what I can for Mary and Henry. Fight for my husband's old sinecure or a pension in its place....'

She was a fighter, there was no doubt. Palmer slipped away to the safety of the Charterhouse.

'Yon boy Davenant is back.'

Palmer was surprised to hear the news from Toby Hume and to find out that Davenant had been in London alone, carrying a new play with him for weeks without making contact.

It was no longer easy for Palmer at seventy to stagger around the town making enquiries and leaving messages for the elusive writer at the Blackfriars and at the Globe and in the alehouses nearby. He got the distinct impression that he was being blocked and avoided.

He had one stratagem left for which he had to borrow half a crown from his Scots friend.

'If he won't come to me I will go to him in a way he can't deny me,' Palmer told Hume as he took the weighty coin.

He made his way to the Blackfriars Playhouse for its afternoon performance of the play of the moment.

'*The Wits* by our William D'Avenant, in which a pair of country gents come to town to pursue the ladies only to find themselves the biters bit.'

This was the playhouse teller's line to all enquirers including Palmer.

He paid his money and had himself hauled up with some difficulty into one of the fashionable seated positions onstage, the sturdiest stool which could be found.

'Who's that bristly old boar?' one of the actors said, looking in from backstage.

Davenant took a look.

'O great God!'

How the audience laughed as the country gallants were locked up in a chest, swindled out of money and jewels and lured into assignations only to be surprised by Snore the constable.

Or more truthfully, how they had begun to laugh until they could see that one man onstage was not enjoying any of the jokes, worse, he was turning his back on them.

Among the sweat and spittle of the actors, Palmer's reaction was becoming the greater joke at the expense of the play. Beyond Palmer, the unseduceable Lady Ample appeared increasingly annoyed – he was not getting his usual laughs at the expense of the country visitors.

'It's Christopher Sly,' a voice from the pit called out, old enough to have seen Shakespeare's *Shrew*, 'dreaming the play.'

Backstage, the actors were in a quandary about what to do.

Snore the constable was the most upset.

'He's ruining my best bits of business!' the old comedian complained to Davenant.

'It's all right,' Davenant sighed, 'just leave him to me, I'll put a stop to it.'

Davenant looked little different to Palmer's eyes when he looked past the man's rich, fashionable dress. They had places to eat in an ordinary nearby to where the playwright had abstracted his problem stage spectator.

'You have a success on your hands,' Palmer said.

'It's my first comedy. It appears to be pleasing the crowd. You know the Master of the Revels was not keen to license it. My friend Mr Endymion Porter was forced to intervene.'

Palmer thought back to his own time in the Revels office. Old Tilney would have brooked no such interference, his successor Buc would have liked the type of play it was. He said as much.

'It cut no ice with stuffy Herbert,' Davenant said. 'Endymion had to take it to the King.'

'The King?'

'Yes, the King read it and called Herbert in. He took him through the text – the problem was with the oaths I flavoured the dialogue with trying to make it sound how people really speak.'

Oaths, swearing, bad language were not good Palmer knew, they had been outlawed onstage in his own time in the Revels together with any representation of important living personalities.

'They were not oaths, the King said, they were ... asseverations.'

A fancy word meaning a serious statement.

Other than how a man prone to stammering got his tongue round the word, Palmer was not impressed. That a reigning monarch should be bothering with a row over a here-today-and-gone-tomorrow comedy seemed to him to be a serious statement of the unserious times.

'Herbert gave way?' he asked.

'Ungraciously. Herbert gave me the text back, as corrected by the King,' he said as if to tell me to my face that it was none of his own doing.'

'So what is next?'

There was bound to be a next.

'The success of the play has returned me not only to the *public* eye.'

Davenant gave Palmer a knowing look.

'Ah ... the Queen?'

A pretty face with protuberant teeth masked behind a fan came back into Palmer's mind, the night when Davenant was first presented to Their Majesties.

'Her Majesty has let it be known,' Davenant confided, not for the first time even if it was to the old man in front of him, 'that she would also like to see a comedy but in the romantic style.'

'Courtly love?' Palmer guessed.

'Platonic, all very platonic.'

The two men looked each other over until Davenant burst out laughing.

'It's what she wants, it's very à la mode. What is it *you* want, Mr Palmer?' he asked more seriously.

'Have you seen your wife and child?'

'I have sent them money as and when it comes to me.'

Palmer saw the expression on the other man's face change.

'For God's sake, Mr Palmer,' Davenant protested, 'how many men live apart from their wives as their business calls them to? Ben Jonson, now, he barely lived with his....'

'Because she was a shrew,' Palmer said and because no one in their right mind could live with that man, ever or especially now, sick, he had heard and bedridden these last few years but still clinging on to his hopes and ambitions, clear in mind if broken in body.

'My fa..., Master Shakespeare, he and his wife spent years apart.'

'Because she was a country wife. Miracle lives in town not one mile separate from you. And don't tell me she is like old Jonson's wife because we both know that's not true.'

'You never married, Mr Palmer.'

'No, I did not.'

He had thought to only once, in the far off days of his youth in Kent, to Emilia. What a lucky escape it had been for both of them. He saw Davenant's point – what did he know about it?

'I married too young, Mr Palmer, we both did, Miracle and I. I've had the pox, life's events have carried me away, tossed me up and now put me down in this place for as long as it lasts. Take any of this back to Miracle and mix it up as you choose, oh, and throw this in for good measure,' Davenant said, tossing a purse across to Palmer.

Palmer pocketed it, his expression unchanged.

~ 17 ~

PALMER TOLD MIRACLE no such thing but he did pass over the purse entire despite temptation to take a cut.

Davenant quickly followed up the success of his *Wits* play with one called *Love and Honour*.

The title did strike Palmer as ironical under the circumstances.

Hume went to see it at the Blackfriars, Palmer did not.

'There's a muckle of folks – lads and lasses both, out'a – what's it called? – aye, chivalry, trying to save this heiress Evandra who's set to have her head chopped clean away by the Duke on account o' her being daughter to another Duke, his mortal foe.'

Did it end well or badly Palmer wanted to know, was it romance or tragedy?

'We-ell, o'course. I was better entertained by a wee story on the side about a soldier forced to marry wi' an auld widow. Was he reckoning to court her with music, he's asked? Na, she's deaf as a post so there's nae cost there!'

Palmer found it hard not to laugh.

The next year brought Davenant his courtly reward.

Palmer heard about it this time from Nicholas Lanier on the coincidence of both paying a visit to Emilia's house in Clerkenwell to see how things were going with Henry Lanier's widow and children who had returned to their family home.

'Master Davenant is well planted in the Court,' Lanier said. 'He has been chosen as Inigo Jones's latest partner for the next masque which will be called *The Temple of Love*. Her Majesty and a dozen of her Ladies will appear....'

Palmer left it to Emilia to ask what the masque was about.

'A temple of chaste love,' Lanier said as seriously as he could manage. 'The Goddess Poetry bids an Indian queen – Her Majesty herself – to create such a place, in which she is opposed by three magicians but she wins the day and so Chaste Love descends from above – cue Master Jones's machine – to bring on *His* Majesty to join his royal wife in....'

'Chastity?' Palmer woke up to enquire. 'Just how many children do Their Majesties have?'

Three at least to his own knowledge.

'And the music,' Emilia asked, 'who writes the music?'

'I am Master of the *King*'s Musick, not the Queen's but I imagine I shall have a hand in it. When old Jonson was Jones's masqueing partner I was more frequently employed.'

Lanier soon left leaving Emilia and Palmer to such talk as they could muster.

'I have won my case against my brother-in-law Clement – the one who took my late husband's sinecure without compensating me.'

'How much?' Palmer asked, determined to avoid a blow-by-blow account.

'Twenty pounds,' Emilia said proudly.

Enough to keep her going for two or three years Palmer calculated.

'Have you got it yet?'

What he got was her 'don't be silly' look. It would become the regular point of conversation between them as she pursued the debt over the coming years.

The masque led to a play, *The Platonic Lovers* also at the Blackfriars, again performed by the King's Men. Hume was Palmer's informant.

'Yon Davenant has the wit to have said what we're all thinking about this form of love. *'But who shall make men? Shall the world cease?'*

Davenant was safely clasped to the Queen's chaste bosom, Palmer could only observe from a distance as the years passed. On the domestic front Henry Lanier's children were growing up healthy as was their older cousin young William Davenant, son of his absent father, unique child of Miracle. Money came to her from her husband in name as and when.

The Banqueting House, Whitehall, erstwhile scene of the masques was closed while the ceilings were fixed with paintings imported from the Flemish studio of one Rubens on whom the irrepressible Hume had only one comment: 'he paints big lassies.' Palmer staggered out of the Charterhouse to see them with Hume to keep him upright, taking several stops along the way across the capital for refreshment.

The subject was a fleshy display in the heroic-religious style of the apotheosis of King James, his elevation into Heaven. Its point was to emphasise the divine right of the Stuart monarchy to rule without the aid of mortal men. More and more of *them* were being provoked to make trouble for the King in or out of Parliament.

Palmer's first reaction was to laugh.

'Do you see the expression on the old King's face as he is being hauled up?'

Hume, who had known the man well shared in the fun.

'Aye, he looks like an auld dog woken up to go out into the winter cold, he disn'a like it.'

At least the painter Rubens had a sense of humour, Palmer liked to think.

There were to be no more masques given here, the pair were told. King Charles feared damage to the paintings from candle-heat, light and smoke 'on the advice of the King's expert' they were also told, 'Master Nicholas Lanier.'

Instead there was to be a new masqueing room built of brick and wood, bigger than the Banqueting House itself in the courtyard behind it. So there was to be no escaping the masques. Only death brought that Palmer reflected when he heard the news that the masque creator- in-chief had died, Ben Jonson in the dog days of August 1637.

Was it thirty years and more since the old bull had been in trouble for sharing supper with the Gunpowder plotters? Would he, Palmer, outlive them all?

1638 found Palmer still alive to his own surprise and Hume likewise to his pleasure.

He was not entirely prepared for what was to be the annus mirabilis of William Davenant or the beginning of events which would send the man's fortunes in the opposite direction.

'Yon Davenant is made Poet Laureate,' Hume told Palmer one day in spring after Chapel.

What did that mean? Palmer asked him.

'A few pretty verses to Their Majesties on occasion an' one hundred poonds per year.'

A hundred pounds a year? Palmer sighed. He'd have settled for a tenth of that in his time but he knew it would not be enough, not for Davenant who had a Court lifestyle to maintain as well as the inconvenience of a wife and child in the world outside.

'Must ha' been that last masque with Inigo Jones that swang it.'

Britannia Triumphans Hume had read and retold to Palmer praised its King for transforming his lands at home and abroad into a hive of goodness and science. The Queen had responded by commissioning the same pair Jones & Davenant to stage her reply *Luminalia* in which she herself appeared dancing with her Ladies on the theme of light and dark.

As if Davenant did not have enough on his hands with the masques he knocked out a couple of plays, the first, *The Unfortunate Lovers* drawing a unique audience when the Queen and Court came out of the palace into the City for the first time ever to see it at the Blackfriars. It was standard Italian revenge play stuff in which the lovers of the title died in each other's arms. This was the word which got back to the two old men in the

Charterhouse. A second play, *The Fair Favourite* was held back for the Court season at Christmas; in it a chaste royal favourite was in the end allowed to love another while her King and lover rediscovered his love for his neglected Queen.

'Life does not imitate his art,' Palmer said to Hume, thinking of Miracle.

'He's certainly busy with his pen.'

Rumour also whispered that Poet Laureate Davenant had come so far that he was arranging to have his portrait painted by a fashionable artist.

'He talks o' Van Dyck but he's getting Greenhill,' was Hume's pithy report.

In addition to two masques, two plays and a portrait Davenant also excited the talk of the town by publishing a collection of forty-two poems entitled *Madagascar*, some of them addressed to his patroness the Queen, others to his perennial friend and mentor Endymion Porter.

Palmer laughed quietly to himself over his dinner in the Great Hall of the Charterhouse. William Shakespeare had once written one hundred and fifty poems and Palmer had been forced to read every one. He had no such intention even with the lighter load in *Madagascar*.

The following year brought the crowning point of Davenant's upward progress – he was authorised to build a theatre behind a popular eating-place off Fleet Street and to recruit a company of actors, dancers and musicians to fill it.

What could go wrong?

The King could.

With his Archbishop, Laud, King Charles decided to impose Anglican bishops and prayerbook on pernickety Scotland.

'Guid luck wi' that,' said Hume when he heard.

The Scots, independent in their Government if not their King replied in the way they generally did to impositions from the south – with action rather than protest. Any bishops imposed would be removed and Presbyterianism restored was their fierce riposte. Such changes as he wanted the King was finding out were more easily commanded in a masque than in real life.

'Aye, it's war,' Hume pronounced without enlightening old Palmer on which side of the argument he stood. 'The King marches north to York.'

More to the surprise of both was who was going with him.

'Assisting the Master of Ordnance?'

Palmer snorted into his cloak when Hume brought him the news of Davenant's military promotion.

'Whatever does he know about guns and ammunition, horses and transport?'

What he turned out to be good at was using carrier pigeons, a one-time play-idea of his to enable correspondence between the King on campaign and his Queen at home. The man was never short of novel ideas.

The whole confused military expedition got as far as Berwick and into the Scottish borders before a truce was signed and then it was turn and turn about dragging the whole train back down to London.

Davenant's reward was to arrive back to find permission for his new theatre withdrawn.

'It's Herbert, the Master of the Revels, he is my enemy,' Davenant explained on a rare visit to his clandestine wife and son when Palmer happened to be with them.

A story of theatrical intrigue came out going back to *The Wits* which Herbert had tried to block – the King himself intervening.

'Herbert has money invested with my rivals in another playhouse,' Davenant finished up by saying.

A childish voice interrupted them.

'When we go to war again can I come with you? I could be your ensign.'

The voice belonged to Davenant's son, young William's, barely broken.

Palmer looked him over. He had the best of his parents' looks, none of his father's bravado and all of his dreaminess. He was just the type to go off to war and get himself killed before his time.

Palmer saw that Davenant saw it too.

'There will be no more war, William,' father told son.

Davenant's mind was back on the theatre.

A play called *The Spanish Lovers*, which was about what it said was to be put into rehearsal for performance in the winter. And why should war put an end to masqueing? Jones & Davenant were soon busy with *Salmacida Spolia* in which a king who loves his people '*rules in adverse times*'.

For the first time King Charles and Queen Henrietta Maria performed alongside each other, showing the select world of the Court that reform and progress was not impossible in the world of the masque.

There was war with the Scots again in the summer of the year following, 1640.

It came highly inconveniently to Davenant who had just been put in – by his mortal enemy Herbert of all people – to run a rival theatre to the one he had hoped to build. It was the one the Master of the Revels was reputed to have money invested in it when its management made the mistake of putting on a play critical of the King and Queen.

'They failed to get Herbert's licence for it,' Davenant gave out, 'which really got his goat. He had to get it taken off despite the effect on his own purse!'

Off went Davenant to the same war, same cause. The professional soldiers involved found reason to grumble about amateurs like him. He turned sharply on them about the lack of money provided to pay for the horses and transport for an artillery train due to be moved by him from Newcastle to Hull.

And he got himself mixed up in what became called the Army Plot.

'WILLIAM DAVENANT, you and others attempted to seduce the Army to act against Parliament before which you now appear. The others named are Henry Percy brother to the Earl of Northumberland, Henry Jermyn an intimate of Her Majesty the Queen, Sir John Suckling like you a scribbler and a fop and Captain Billingsley, soldier.'

Toby Hume was in attendance to hear the charge. When he reported these names to Palmer the old investigator sucked on the few teeth he had left. Old names kept coming round. The Percys for example had been mixed up in the Gunpowder plot against King James and in the Essex rebellion.

'What did our man have to say for himself?' Palmer asked.

'He said that all that was laid agin him were no' but suspicions and opinions, that he might ha' spoken rashly, used ill-conceived words at table but without serious intent, oh, and mebbe the same in writing, rash words but never, what was it? "Irreverently or maliciously".'

Palmer nearly laughed. Hume was not put off.

'He did say that he himself had written to Her Majesty with the notion that she become the People's voice to bend His Majesty's gracious will more to the changing times. And I will say this, the laddie made his case wi' an ingratiating charm such as no mon could hate him.'

Palmer bet he did.

'And he got off?'

'Bail on sureties of four thousand poond, half of that from hissel'.'

Palmer whistled at the amount. If Davenant could lay his hands on two thousand pounds....

'The die ... *is* cast, Mr Palmer, or are?'

'It's plural in the original Latin, William.'

Both men were sat at the table of Miracle and her son, a place Davenant had frequented more and more since his troubles with Parliament. It was a homecoming of sorts.

'The world is full of inflexible people. The Parliament men really are the devils....'

'And the King is not?'

The voice was Miracle's.

'You may be right, but a man is loyal to his tribe....'

Davenant looked meaningfully at his son as he said it.

'.... and above all to his friends. Their Majesties have been good to me and to us. What do these Puritans offer us? As Master Shakespeare told us they think there shall be no cakes and ale if they have their way and then where would we poor poets be?'

'Are there no Puritan poets?' his son asked him.

'If there are they're poor ones, hymn writers and the like. I'll grant you John Milton but he's the exception that proves the rule *if* you like his antique bombasting style.'

'London is loyal to Parliament,' Palmer said gruffly.

'I know but London isn't all the world. If King and Commons clash mortally, will you stay in the Charterhouse?'

'Where else would I go at my age? But where will the King go?'

Davenant looked around him as if suspecting spies lurking in the shadows around them.

'To where his loyal friends are.'

'As the King's friend will you go with him?'

Miracle asked the vital question.

Davenant looked at his wife and then his son.

'I must.'

Davenant's performance before Parliament worked because, while three of the five accused were found guilty of treason Davenant's case was left as at best inconclusive, 'not proven' as Hume, borrowing from Scots Law put it. It came as a surprise to Palmer who had seen State treason trials before. The guilty verdict was usually guaranteed well before the opening statements.

In January 1642 King Charles made his reckless and unsuccessful attempt to arrest the five leaders of the Parliamentary faction opposing him in the House of Commons against all procedure and protocol.

Days later Palmer heard that Miracle Davenant had been brought to bed of a daughter Mary. He was surprised and he wasn't. Davenant was a man of warm affections and there was little at Court, nothing in the theatre and nobody in either to draw his wandering eye.

Politics and another bout of the plague made sure of that. And when the playhouses were allowed to re-open the Puritans in Parliament complained against them. The writing was on the wall.

The King ran north to raise his standard in Nottingham, the Queen to the continent. Davenant went with her to raise money for the cause. Miracle and her little family were left to shift as best they could.

The Puritans got their way over the playhouses. It had been coming for as long as he could remember Palmer told Hume, the middling classes opposed to the tastes of their apprentices and their betters at Court who were all for roistering at play during the working day and, despite prohibition, on the Sabbath too if they could get away with it.

'The ban is temp'ry they say,' said Hume.

Palmer gave him his most sceptical look.

'Aye well, ye're mebbe right – the actors are gan, run off out o' toon to His Majesty. They've sold their playbooks and their fancy costumes and all. I've a mind to ga maself. I'm barely sixty, there's older men fighting for the cause.'

If Palmer didn't believe him, sight of a draft petition by Hume convinced him.

'My scheme is to subdue the rebels in Ireland and, if I'm given command o' a fleet, to bring in twenty million pounds for the King inside three months! Wadda ye think?' he asked Palmer. 'D'ye think the figure a wee bit steep?'

Palmer examined the text through fading eyes. There was no point disillusioning his old friend; he must be going soft in the brain.

'You've signed it Captain Hume.'

'As I am, as I was.'

'Captains are ten a penny and most of them counterfeit. Promote yourself or who will believe you?'

'To what?'

'To Colonel.'

Hume got no reply and therefore no exeat from the Charterhouse. London remained under Parliament's control and opposed to the King.

The two old veterans were left to study what news they could get whether by reading between the lines in the *Mercurius Britanicus* the Parliamentary news-sheet or by word of mouth.

'Davenant's in the north as General of Ordnance.'

Palmer kept this news to the seclusion of Hume's room because the Charterhouse had a long record of loyalty to the Crown but you never could tell where individual loyalties lay. Word was that the authorities in the Hospital were already making friends within Parliament which was holding London against the King. A lot more whispering was going on in little cliques at table, in Chapel and around the building.

'That'll mean Davenant's working under Newcastle.'

The Earl of Newcastle was the King's Lord General, another former gentleman playwright at the Blackfriars which was a point not missed by the critics of either man, Newcastle or Davenant.

A story smuggled through the lines to Miracle amused the pair of ancients cocooned from events in the former monastery. Davenant had been put in charge of a pair of captured Alderman from York. He judged it easier to connive with them in their escape, which they did – only they came back to thank him out of good manners before he could get rid of them for a second time on their way to freedom.

It sounded very Davenant.

'There's been a great battle at Edgehill in the west,' Hume announced to Palmer. 'Parliament is defeated, the King and his forces ha'e marched triumphant into Oxford.'

The news made London, seat of Parliament a much uneasier place.

Months later and 'the Queen has joined the King, carrying wi' her a muckle o' money raised abroad'.

She had been escorted through Stratford-upon-Avon where she was lodged in New Place, royal guest of Widow Hall, Susanna Shakespeare as was. Her father had been a King's Man after all. So Susanna had her wish, Palmer remembered from the dinner conversation with her years ago.

The same day Miracle came to visit her old godfather.

'I've had word from William,' she said. 'We're to join him, the King and the Queen in Oxford.'

She could barely suppress her excitement. Palmer looked her up and down, a woman not yet forty; was she pregnant again?

'How will you do that?'

She knew what he meant. There was commerce around the kingdom but passes and permissions were now needed especially to enter or leave London.

'I have family in Oxford,' she said.

Palmer remembered them, especially the jealous foster-sister Jane, landlady of the Crown Tavern.

'Jane's a widow now as I will be unless I make this move.'

'So you're the guardian, are you?'

The official looked suspiciously at the old wreck in the Charterhouse cloak standing or trying to in front of him.

'Godfather, in loco parentis inter alia.'

Palmer was speculating that the man in front of him had no Latin and would respect anyone who had.

'The lady and her children have no family here, they are Oxford people originally and have family there. As you can see I'm a gentleman-pensioner, I'm not able to look after them. They will only become a charge, a charge on the parish unless they are allowed to go.'

London already had too many incomers due to the current hostilities.

'Where's the 'usband?'

'Abandoned them a long time ago. Likely dead, a complete wastrel, a player.'

Palmer liked to keep as close to the truth as possible.

'And *you're* going to escort them?'

The man's incredulity was tangible.

'Sure you're not runnin' away to fight for the King?!'

Palmer growled a denial. What would break the impasse?

'What's their name?' the official asked.

'Davenant,' Palmer said.

'Now 'old on, that's a name I know.'

'It's a common one, in Oxford they're, um, tavern folk.'

'So 'ow would I know that name, of tavern folk in Oxford when I've never been there?'

Palmer sighed.

'You may be thinking of General Davenant, the royalist officer.'

'Yes that' s it!'

'Unrelated or if so distantly. This lady is a tavern-keeper's daughter.'

Palmer leaned closer to whisper.

'Mother ran away and ended up a whore in Clerkenwell.'

Not untrue, he told himself. He dealt his last card.

'I imagine these passes are an expensive business. Will this defray the cost?'

Palmer showed the man a half crown and saw the light of avarice in his eyes.

'Well yes, that will cover it, just about.'

Palmer took Miracle, her son William and the baby Mary out of the City's western wall through Ludgate. He stayed with them as far as Tyburn Tree within reach of the Oxford road. By far the hardest part had been to find a party permitted to travel to Oxford with the necessary protection for the rigours of the road made worse by the state of war.

Palmer and Miracle looked at each other, both thinking the same thing. Eighty next birthday, Palmer reminded himself. He was determined to make it in order to outstrip Benefactor Sutton of the Charterhouse to the annoyance of the Hospital's authorities

He saw tears welling up in Miracle's eyes. He hated tears. The last he had shed was when the Palmers had been evicted from their ancestral home a lifetime ago. He had made a vow then never to cry again. He was finding it hard to keep.

He opened his arms and clasped his goddaughter closely enough to satisfy her needs. He watched her go, waving as she disappeared into the distance.

Getting back into the City wasn't going to be easy.

The sight of an old man stumbling his way back east, aided by a couple of spare pennies got him hoisted, with difficulty onto the unlatched tailgate of a passing cart. The open road from Oxford leading into town took him through open fields grazed by cows and sheep. Trees masked the suburban village of St Giles to his right. It was many years since he had come this way bringing in the Gunpowder plotters and before them, the errant playwright Shakespeare mixed up in a play to get the mob in the mood for regicide. The village appeared bigger, more prosperous, more houses lining its streets.

On the left, in its own grounds stood what had been Southampton House.

Dead more than twenty years, the beautiful youth of all those sonnets, the old man dozing on the back of the cart half-dreamed, old times coming more easily to his mind and driving out the present difficulties.

Holborn was busier, the suburb giving way to the city. Ely House stretched out on Palmer's left, once home of the young Davenant's Double Duchess. She was dead, bless her, on the eve of the wars.

At Holborn Bridge over the stinking Fleet the cart was held up for inspection a few hundred yards short of Palmer's destination.

'I've run away from the Charterhouse,' Palmer joked with the man asking for his credentials. 'I expect they'll be out looking for me.'

Rumour gave out that the newly knighted Sir William D'Avenant was travelling on the continent raising money for the royal cause when he wasn't writing – sombre poems of consolation to his royal mistress from across the sea while her husband fought on in England.

Paris and Amsterdam were talked of as his whereabouts.

Meantime Parliamentary victories threatened Oxford and the threat sent the Queen out west and across the sea into exile in her native France, never to see her husband again.

The Globe Theatre, closed two years past was pulled down to make way for tenement housing.

'*All the world's a stage?*'

Not any more it wasn't.

'Oy, Methusaleh – both of yer! We 'asn't got all day!'

The impatience of the boatman did nothing to improve the steadiness of Palmer or Hume struggling into the waiting boat on the Thames, or over on the opposite bank when they finally got there.

Sounds of building work drew Palmer on, followed by Hume, slower in his movements these last few weeks. Hammering, sawing, creaking cartwheels and the calls and curses of workmen brought the two ancients to the spot.

The Globe Theatre stood in front of them, already half taken down. The roof was off and most of the plasterwork piled up in dumps open to scavengers or to be carted away further downriver. Surviving upright timbers pointed accusing fingers at a leaden sky; others stood stacked or lay packed in neat piles ready for re-use in a new building.

Palmer took in the scene. Blurred memories in sight and sound crowded in on him, very little of the actors and their one-time traffic on a stage already dismantled in front of him, more the flashes of curious, half-forgotten events – the Alderman's wife and friends hanging out of their gallery as Ned Shakespeare strutted his stuff below, goatish Simon Forman laying in wait to practise his sententious morals drawn from the plays, Cecil's old official tongue-tied in the presence of the actors – Burbage, Hemmings, Condell – backstage in the busy commerce of the tiring house; and William Shakespeare himself, evasive, evanescent as the circumstances dictated behind the scenes or there onstage, taking the action forward, never to be nailed down. To Palmer, his spirit hovered over the place, genius loci, he smiled to himself, now thinking of Miracle in the churchyard where her mother Ellen lay buried. Where were they all now? Down in the dust, down in the dust.

The old alehouse nearby tempted him but he turned his back on it and guided Hume back to the river.

Not long after, Hume died – 'young Hume' as Palmer had taken to calling him because he was fifteen years younger.

Palmer pulled his cloak tighter around him.

And then Emilia the indestructible fell onto her deathbed. Palmer went unwillingly to say farewell, bandages strapped round his legs to enable him to stump along to her little house.

He was not alone. A half-recognised figure passed him going out on his way in, old and grizzled just as he was. He wracked his brains as to who it was without finding an answer.

'Who was that?' he asked the slight form unmoving in the bed.

No answer came at first then a feeble voice.

'He promises he will say...'

The word 'kaddish' was lost on the visitor. Pulling up a stool to the bedside, Palmer was about to ask what she meant when he remembered how he knew the departing figure, an ancient version of the Deptford chandler, a man from another race about whose customs, her customs he knew nothing.

'They have all come.'

Who, he asked?

'The priests, from St James's....'

Where else?

'... and from the ... the old faith. For the last rites and ... prayers ... prayers when I am gone.'

Palmer was struck by Emilia's appetite, this time for salvation. She was calling in all the prayers she could from every quarter. When his time came Palmer hoped for sleep and undisturbed rest, a theme which had once exercised a man of words they both knew well in other times.

... to sleep, perchance to dream, he muttered to himself, hoping not.

Time passed, marked by the closing in of the light as day began to fail.

Palmer heard a stirring in the bed.

'Who are you?'

'An old friend,' Palmer said remembering the days of Kent and a young woman playing her keyboard hard enough to blot out the nonsenses of love he had wanted to ply her with.

'A friend?'

There was a plaint in the voice he couldn't bear. Silence. A soft whistling sound replaced it, the last sleep before extinction.

Palmer waited until the last breath, a sigh and then nothing more. He touched her hand and left her simulacrum, to tell the priest in St James's.

Palmer went to neither funeral, Hume's or Emilia's. He pleaded infirmity of body even if the truth was that it was more of purpose.

He did not recognise the brother who brought him a letter one day into his room where he had taken refuge. His legs would carry him no further.

He waited until he was alone before he opened it. He used Hume's old spyglass to read it.

'Uncle Two Names,

We are safe where you sent us....'

Clever girl, Palmer thought, careful with the information she disclosed.

'... my sister Jane looks after us....'

Palmer searched his failing memory until he found her, a flighty young woman set on marrying the Tavern apprentice and seeing her foster-sister off the premises. Twenty years of tavern-keeping and widowhood had obviously converted her to greater family kindness.

'... myself, William, baby John – named after his grandfather, my husband's father....'

Laconic John Davenant from Gunpowder days stood promptly in Palmer's mind's eye as if it was yesterday.

'... and another child due, to be called Richard if it's a boy, after you....'

Palmer felt the pricking of unwelcome tears.

'... my husband is away a great deal but I want you to know, dear godfather, that we are more united than ever, even than in the days of our youth. The present times have brought their consolations. Here where I am....'

Oxford, Palmer said to himself, unstated, but Oxford.

'... in my end is my beginning....'

End, what end?

Palmer put the letter down. Only with reluctance did he pick it up again.

'I have given instructions that this letter be sent to you in the hope that you are God willing still living and in the Charterhouse. You will receive it in the event....'

What event? A horrible, clammy fear began to grip the old man.

'... that my confinement and the coming into the world of little Richard, as I hope he will be, becomes my own end here in the place of my beginning.'

Palmer remembered the cool river on a hot summer's day and a newborn brought to life by his own rough baptising.

His eyes returned to the script signed in strong strokes of the pen by a dead woman.

The last of the Palmers turned his face to the wall.

~ Closing the File ~

EMILIA LANIER was buried in the churchyard of St James's, Clerkenwell in an unmarked grave. There is no record of Palmer's last resting place, in the Charterhouse we must presume.

Sir William D'Avenant as he styled himself survived the English Civil War in which he played a busy part and converted to Catholicism. He lost his eldest son William who died young in the Oxford tavern kept by his sister Jane. His daughter Mary married a prelate who was uncle to the satirist Jonathan Swift. His other possible children by this marriage, John and Richard leave no mark of reaching adulthood.

On 30 January 1649, King Charles I stepped out of the Banqueting House, Whitehall, scene of his masque dancing from under the painted ceiling showing the elevation of his father King James into Heaven onto the scaffold where he was executed by verdict of a Parliamentary trial. He was wearing two shirts against the cold to prevent any shivering being interpreted as fear. His supporters claimed martyrdom and later sainthood for him. Queen Henrietta Maria did see London again on her son Charles II's restoration when she tried to break the engagement of her second son James, Duke of York to a daughter of the statesman Edward Hyde who once gave lodging to Davenant in Middle Temple. Their daughters became in succession Queens Mary and Anne bringing to an end the Stuart line.

Davenant's mentor Endymion Porter died in penury in London in the same year as King Charles I. Davenant

Two years later, a Lady Bernard died in Northamptonshire. Elizabeth, sole surviving grandchild of William Shakespeare, twice married, childless, closed the Shakespeare line.

www.ingramcontent.com/pod-product-compliance
Lightning Source LLC
Chambersburg PA
CBHW050739180626
46814CB00002B/826